CASSIE EDWARDS

SAVAGE SUN

LEISURE BOOKS NEW YORK CITY

A LEISURE BOOK®

April 2009

Published by

Dorchester Publishing Co., Inc.
200 Madison Avenue
New York, NY 10016

ISBN 10: 0-8439-5879-0
ISBN 13: 978-0-8439-5879-9
E-ISBN: 1-4285-0647-0

The name "Leisure Books" and the stylized "L" with design are trademarks of Dorchester Publishing Co., Inc.

Printed in the United States of America.

10 9 8 7 6 5 4 3 2 1

Visit us on the web at www.dorchesterpub.com.

An Intriguing Prospect

"You call me son now, when you want something
from me?" Tall Moon said, interrupting his father
once again. "Or was that a slip of the tongue?"

"Tall Moon, let me speak without interrupting me," Lawrence said. "All I want are the trees.
Surely that isn't a problem, is it?"

To Tall Moon it definitely was a problem, but he
felt that this wasn't the time to tell his father that he
wasn't welcome to cut the majestic cypress elms in
the swamp. And Tall Moon did not wish to argue
in the presence of this woman. He had been very
aware of the way she was looking at him, curiosity
shining from her beautiful blue eyes.

Of course, she had probably never been this close
to an Indian before. He could not help wondering
what she was thinking as she stood there, looking
at him in such a way.

He hoped that she was not afraid of Indians. Then
he chided himself.

He knew that he shouldn't care what she
thought.

But deep inside himself, he did care, for he had to
admit he was intrigued by her.

SAVAGE SUN

Chapter One

Arkansas—1871

The White River carved its way through the pristine wilderness, its clear water flowing beneath the outspread branches of September elms, wild magnolias and sassafras.

A canoe, carrying a lone Indian in it, moved slowly and silently through the water. Tall Moon, a young *uku* chief of twenty-eight winters, was looking for the perfect place to stop and fish. Having begun his meal with berries and hazelnuts that he had found in the forest, he hoped to end it with a tasty trout or catfish.

He was from the *Ani-dji-skwa*, the Bird Clan of the Cherokee. He was muscled and tall and had waist-length black hair that flowed down his back like a river at midnight. His flashing dark eyes were always alert, with vision as sharp as a hawk's. Today he wore his usual attire of breechclout and moccasins made from the skins of beavers.

Tall Moon smiled as he moved slowly through the water in his canoe, for today life was good. He loved the peaceful feeling of the river, where the only movement was of forest animals such as the white-tailed deer. He spotted some standing at the riverbank, drinking from the river and feasting on the delicious berries as he had done.

Such sights as this always filled Tall Moon's heart with a gentle peace.

But suddenly that peace was broken.

The hair bristled at the nape of his neck and he yanked his paddle from the water when he heard the loud thud of trees being felled. The sound was like thunder as the trunks crashed hard against the earth.

Until now, no one but his own people had inhabited this remote part of Arkansas. Fleeing the wrath of the white people's government, he had led his people to this swampland, believing it a place where white people would not want to make their homes. The *Ani-dji-skwa* had made do, building their homes on a stretch of land that was close to the swamp, alongside the White River.

Tall Moon hated to think that he might have to uproot his people again to avoid these men who had come to the swamp to fell trees so close to his home. He had no wish to leave the river that provided the Bird Clan with small mouth bass, catfish, and trout, the basic foods they depended on.

The river gave his people not only food for their cook fires, but also sustenance for their souls. They all enjoyed paddling their canoes beneath the beautiful limestone bluffs that towered overhead.

He had stopped one day, himself, and ventured through the hidden caverns, in awe of how nature had carved such mighty places out of stone.

Again he heard the thunder of another tree falling to the ground in the nearby swamp. As his canoe drifted closer to the sounds of destruction, Tall Moon could clearly hear the voices of those who had came uninvited to this place to fell trees that should have been left untouched forever. He was certain it was white men who were cutting the huge cypress elms that grew in the swamp so close to his people's home. He was equally certain these white men must be made to leave.

But he knew that he could not deal with this threat alone. He must return home to tell his warriors of the white men's arrival and to plan a strategy to drive them off.

He turned his canoe around and began paddling away from the threat that had come upon his people.

Ho, yes, he did feel threatened for the first time since he had led his people into hiding here. Until now, no white man had ventured to this forest. The dangers and mysteries of the swampland made it undesirable for white people's settlements.

It was not land that whites fought and killed for. But Tall Moon's people had made it work for them.

But now?

It seemed history was repeating itself. Once again, whites were dangerously close to his home.

Not so long ago, many of his Cherokee clan had died during skirmishes with white soldiers, who seemed determined to rid the entire land of all men with red skins.

Tall Moon had led his clan to safety in Arkansas after the white soldiers had forced them off their ancestral lands in Georgia. The whites had planned to send all the Cherokee to a reservation in Oklahoma, but Tall Moon had managed to hide his people safely away.

When Tall Moon thought about those who had died during those earlier skirmishes, people who were near and dear to his heart, he fought against bitterness and despair. He must hold those feelings at bay if he was to keep what remained of his Bird Clan alive.

Too many had died under his grandfather's leadership. Tall Moon, who became his people's leader after the death of his grandfather, had survived to make things right for those who lived.

And he would continue to make life good for his people! He had not failed them yet, and he would not now.

Never would he allow the *ha-ha-na*, the enemy, to overcome the *Ani-dji-skwa*.

Chapter Two

The lovely, quaint inn sat in the midst of tall oaks, the only establishment along this stretch of deserted road. The moon was full, pouring its white sheen through the window of her room, as Rowena Dowell gazed out, listening to the croaking of frogs in the nearby river.

The sound took her back in time, to those sweet evenings when she would stand at her bedroom window, listening to the beautiful, soothing sounds of night in her home just outside Atlanta, Georgia.

It seemed oh, so long ago when she had been carefree and happy. Actually, she had lost count of time since she had been sent from her home to live in a convent after the Civil War broke out.

It had almost broken her heart when her father had volunteered to fight for the South. So many men had already died. She'd known there was a good chance her father would never come home again.

With her mother dead and the family's servants run off, her father had sent his only child to live in a convent until the war's end.

But the end of the fighting had not brought an

end to Rowena's troubles. The South had lost the war, her family's plantation home and cotton fields had been burned and left in ruin, and worst of all, during one of the fiercest battles, her father had died from a mortal gunshot wound in his chest.

Tears sprang to her eyes as she recalled her last time with her beloved father. She had wanted their embrace to go on forever, but it was only seconds before he had left her standing at the door of the convent.

When he had walked away, the image of his stout, muscled body and proudly lifted chin had been etched in Rowena's memory forever, as leaves sometimes become fossilized into stone.

Her father had not turned back for a last wave, for Rowena knew that it would be too hard for him to do, as it was hard for her to turn her back on him and walk inside the convent, where the sweet nuns waited to console her.

Her father's passing had broken Rowena's heart into what seemed a million pieces, and his death was the reason she was traveling to Arkansas.

One of the nuns, a gentle old soul, had told her of his passing and the provisions he'd made for her. As her father had lain there on the battlefield, fatally wounded by a bullet that had been meant for his best friend, Lawrence Ashton, he had made a dying request. If Lawrence should live through the battle, would he take Rowena from the convent and look out her? Would he allow Rowena to live with him?

Lawrence's plantation had adjoined Rowena's family's. Ashton had joined the cavalry with her father, to fight for the Confederacy alongside his best friend.

Lawrence Ashton had promised Rowena's father that he would send for Rowena if he was still alive when the war was over. If he wasn't, his son would see to her welfare . . . a son who had not been strong enough to fight for the Confederacy.

Several months after the war ended, Lawrence Ashton had sent word to the convent about Rowena. He had said in his message that Rowena had a home with Lawrence and his son for as long as she wished. Rowena had also been told that Lawrence and his son no longer lived in Atlanta, but in Arkansas.

Where this kind man and his son made their home didn't matter to Rowena. The main thing was that she would no longer be alone in the world.

Despite her gratitude, she couldn't help being uneasy about the fact that she would be living with two men. She had never known Lawrence Ashton's wife, who had died before Rowena was born, but rumor had it that she had been an Indian.

Rowena went to a full-length mirror that hung on the wall opposite the bed. She gazed at herself in it, wondering if she would see the effects of all the tragedy she'd known.

By the lamp that sat on a nightstand beside the bed, Rowena could see that although she felt so much older than she had been before the war, she had not actually changed all that much.

True, there was a more mature look on her oval face, and her blue eyes revealed a trace of sadness over her losses. But otherwise, she was still that petite young lady with the long, flowing golden hair that her father had hugged before leaving her, forever.

She turned and went to the bed, then gently drew the blanket back away from the pillows. She stretched and yawned, knowing that the bed would feel so good after her long day of travel in the stagecoach.

Then again she thought about Lawrence Ashton. She could hardly believe he had abandoned his plantation outside Atlanta. Why hadn't he returned to his true homeland to rebuild what had been destroyed by the Yankees?

She had no idea why he was in Arkansas, but she would find out tomorrow when she arrived there.

She sat on the edge of the bed and removed her shoes, and then her stockings. She did feel so blessed to have someone who cared enough for her to see to her welfare.

But there was one thing that troubled her. She wasn't anxious to see Darren Ashton again. He had never hidden his feelings for her when they were neighbors. She had put him in his place more than once!

She had always thought Darren an arrogant, worthless son of a gun.

Surely now that he was older, he was even worse!

She glanced over at a bench upon which she had laid her violin case. Her precious violin and a few clothes were the only personal belongings that she had left of her past.

Before the war it had been her dream to play in

an orchestra one day, but now even that dream had been dashed.

At least she still had her violin to play for her own pleasure, which she did, often. While she played her instrument, all of her woes disappeared and happiness seemed to bubble up inside her.

Those times were like precious gold to her.

She rolled up her sockings in a tight ball and placed it in one of her shoes, then went barefoot across the cold oak floor to her violin case.

She opened it and gazed lovingly down at the beautiful wooden instrument. She ached to play it now, but she knew that she shouldn't. The sound would awaken people at the inn and she knew that the other travelers needed rest before they headed out again tomorrow to continue their journeys.

She ran her hand over the varnished wood of her violin, tears filling her eyes at the recollection of how her mother and father used to love to hear her play. That, too, was now a part of her past.

Now she must focus on her future and what she could make of it. But first, she must arrive at Lawrence Ashton's home.

She closed her violin case, then went to the window again and gazed out into the moonlit night. She watched dancing shadows in the tall oak forest that stretched out just beyond the inn.

She closed her eyes and envisioned herself back at her home in Atlanta, listening to the night sounds, reveling in them as she had done so often when she was a girl with dreams that would never come true.

But she had not known that then.

The war. That ugly, horrible war had changed her life forever.

She hoped that people had learned something from its horror and would make certain no more such conflicts would tear so many lives asunder.

Chapter Three

After thinking about the arrival of the *ha-ha-na* intruders on Cherokee land, Tall Moon had returned to the place where he had heard the falling trees the day before. Yesterday he had been in his canoe, but today he rode a white stallion he had named Magic.

He felt that he would be too vulnerable in the water, whereas on his horse he could get away much more quickly if there was trouble.

Dressed in fringed buckskin, and armed with his bow and quiver of arrows, he rode slowly beside the White River, watching ahead through breaks in the trees for those who had been cutting the trees yesterday.

After considering the matter, he had decided not to share with his people the news that trouble had possibly come into their lives. He hoped to stop it before he even had to talk to his people about the arrival of the white men. He was returning today to investigate more carefully.

He truly didn't want to alarm his people unless it became necessary. He would prefer to take care of this himself, somehow.

He had chosen to bring his trusted bow today and his quiver of arrows in case he needed protection. If he came across any white men and they threatened him, he would not hesitate to use his bow. An arrow killed silently and would not alert others that he was near.

His bow was slung across his right shoulder. The quiver, filled with the deadly arrows that had been made by his own hand, was strapped to his back.

Today he hoped that he would not be forced to use his weapons. Tall Moon wanted peace, not war!

Remaining hidden among the trees, he now caught sight of several white men on a raft in the river. Drawing cautiously closer, he studied the raft.

It was piled high with freshly cut logs. Seeing them, he could only conclude that these men were allied with those he had heard felling trees yesterday.

They were obviously unaware of being watched, for they continued poling their way down the river.

Tall Moon followed and watched.

He stiffened when the white men thrust their poles into the river and pushed, heading the raft toward shore.

Tall Moon realized that the men were now in the exact spot where he had been yesterday in his canoe when he'd heard the sound of trees crashing to earth.

He drew rein, deciding that he must not venture any closer, for the raft was now beached.

His eyes narrowed angrily as he watched the logs being unloaded from the raft. Chains were attached to the logs, which were then hauled to shore by mules that had been led there by other white men.

He gripped his bow tightly as he watched the mules dragging the logs away from the river. Not able to see enough from his vantage point, Tall Moon quickly dismounted.

He tethered his horse to a low tree limb, then ran softly over the thick cushion of fallen leaves beneath his feet.

He stopped, breathless, when he saw a strange building unlike any he had ever seen before. It had been built with only three sides; the fourth side, which faced the river, had been left open.

His eyes followed the mules as they arrived at the building. The logs were unloaded there and soon sawed by other white men into slabs of wood.

He scarcely breathed as he watched the prepared slabs of wood being piled on another raft in the river and secured with chains. He then watched several men board that raft, standing on each side of the prepared slabs of wood, and begin poling their way upriver.

Suddenly Tall Moon caught movement from the corner of his eye.

He made a quick turn and his eyes widened with disbelief when he saw the person who was arriving at the three-sided shed. It was someone he knew. A face that had once been so very familiar, and one he had thought never to see again.

Although he had not seen his *ah-te*, his father, since he was eight winters of age, he would still know him anywhere.

His *ah-te* was a tall, slim man. He looked the same as Tall Moon remembered him, with two major exceptions. His hair, which had at one time been the color of flame, was now gray, and he had only one arm.

Although Tall Moon still felt the same resentment toward his *ah-te* that he had experienced on that day when his father had cast Tall Moon aside, he could not help being saddened by what had happened to him. This man, who had always been so proud, now seemed to carry the weight of the world on his broad shoulders.

Surely these changes in his father were a result of the war. It had taken much from him . . . his arm, his youthfulness, and now, apparently, also his wealth.

His father had owned a huge cotton plantation just outside Atlanta, Georgia, with many slaves working for him before the war began. He had been rich.

Ho, it was obvious that the war had changed everything. Tall Moon had heard about what had happened to most homes in the South during the war. He supposed that his *ah-te*'s home had been burned, too, by the northern soldiers who came raging across the land.

But it seemed his father had had enough money left to start a lumber business, for Tall Moon noted that his father was giving orders to the men, just as he had once done with his slaves. It seemed clear that these men were his father's laborers.

Then another thought came to Tall Moon. If his *ah-te* was there, where was his *a-na-da-ni-ti*? Had his brother fought and died during the war?

No. He suddenly saw another man and knew it must be his younger brother. He was dressed in better attire than the lumberjacks, and he was standing beside Tall Moon's father, listening, while the others stood facing them, cringing, as orders were being barked at them.

Ho, his brother would be twenty now, eight winters younger than he. He closely resembled their father, with his pale skin, brilliant red hair, and green eyes.

Tall Moon was thrown back in time to when his beloved mother had given birth to a second son by her white husband. Once again he experienced the terrible sense of loss he'd known when giving birth to that son had caused her to lose her life.

She had been a full-blood Cherokee, a princess to their Bird Clan. She had happened to be walking alongside a road one day when his father saw her and was struck by her radiant beauty.

He had been smitten by her. He had looked past the color of her skin. He hadn't cared that she was Indian, and she hadn't cared that he was white.

They had both fallen in love at first glance and were married a short time later.

His mother had given up her birthright, her life as a Cherokee princess, to live as the wife of a wealthy white plantation owner. But she had never forgotten where she came from.

When Tall Moon was born, with all the features of his Cherokee heritage, she had seen the resentment in her husband's eyes. And when she began teaching their son her Indian ways, her husband had quickly forbidden her to continue.

Despite her husband's wishes, his mother had taught Tall Moon everything she felt he should know, in secrecy.

Tall Moon, called Thomas while living with his white father, had been happy enough until his life was turned upside down when his mother died while giving birth to her second child. This son, who so closely resembled his father, would not be an embarrassment to Lawrence Ashton.

Not long after his mother's death, Tall Moon was sent away to live among his Cherokee people, while his white brother stayed with their father and was raised without any knowledge of his Indian heritage.

And that was twenty winters ago.

Tall Moon was now uncertain about whether or not to make himself known to his father and brother.

His father surely had no idea that his wife's people had settled in this part of Arkansas. He had done nothing when the Cherokee were removed from their land and sent to live on what was called reservations.

Tall Moon, who had been taken in by his Cherokee grandparents, had never seen his father since Lawrence Ashton had sent him away.

His grandfather, chief of their clan, had raised Tall Moon to manhood. When he died, Tall Moon was named chief.

Faced with the threat of the white soldiers in Georgia, Tall Moon had cleverly moved his Bird Clan to a strip of land that was useless to whites . . . a swampy area where he'd thought no whites would ever come. He'd been right, until now.

How ironic it was that his own father should be the one who might be the ruination of Tall Moon's people's happiness.

It made no difference that this man was his *ah-te*. Tall Moon had no choice but to see that his plans were stopped.

But he knew that he must not act rashly. The safety of his Cherokee people was at stake.

He started to leave, before someone noticed his presence, but stopped when he saw the arrival of a stagecoach. He watched as a white woman with golden hair stepped daintily down from the coach.

His curiosity aroused, he wondered what in the world she could be doing in such a remote place. He had not seen any other women in his father's camp, only men.

And she was so young; so beautiful; so tiny. Tall Moon thought she must be about eighteen winters of age.

When both his brother and father greeted her warmly, Tall Moon knew that she was someone special to them. But what was the exact nature of their relationship to her?

What role did this beautiful young woman play in their lives?

He knew two things for sure. He wanted to see her again, and he wanted to make certain that this vulnerable beauty was not hurt by Lawrence Ashton or his son Darren.

Chapter Four

As the stagecoach drove away, Lawrence grabbed Rowena's lone travel bag, while she picked up her violin case from the ground where the stagecoach driver had put it.

Lawrence nodded toward the steps that led to a wide porch wrapping around the log cabin on three sides.

"Come on, Rowena," he said, smiling at her over his shoulder. "Let's go inside. The night chill is just beginning to take hold."

He continued smiling at her as she came up beside him while ascending the steps. "You'll get used to it," he said. "Living so close to the swamp, it gets cool and damp at night. There's fog. Oh, my Lord, Rowena, wait until you see how the fog comes swirling in from that damn place. If I didn't have my business established here, I'd go elsewhere. But as it is, the logging is already bringin' in some good dollars. I'll never be a rich man again, but it'll be a comfortable life that I'm offering you, that's for sure."

"I cannot thank you enough for taking me in,"

Rowena murmured as she quickly assessed the house.

Constructed of logs, it was massive and two-storied. Lamplight shining from the windows lent the building a warm and inviting look.

Rowena had felt uncomfortable while Darren was with them, because he had stared at her in an inappropriately intimate fashion, but he had soon excused himself, riding away on his horse. She felt at ease now, confident she would be able to live there until she decided what to do with her future.

More than once, while she was on her journey to Arkansas, she had found herself wondering whether or not she would eventually find her way back to Atlanta, to take over the property that had been her father's pride and joy. It would be wonderful if she could somehow rebuild the plantation.

But she feared that she would be too lonely there without her mother and father. Oh, how she longed for companionship and family.

Her only hope, where loneliness was concerned, was that she might find a gentleman someday who would take a liking to her. For the last four years she had been living in the convent where no men ventured except for priests.

But in time, she hoped to find a normal kind of life again. Until then, this place would have to do, and she did feel so grateful to Lawrence Ashton for having taken her in.

She hoped that her father was looking down from the heavens above and seeing that Lawrence had kept his word. He had given his best friend's daughter a home.

The front door suddenly opened.

The lamplight glowing from within the house revealed a tall, lean black man standing there.

"And this is Amos," Lawrence said, again smiling. "Amos, this is the sweet thing I told you about. This here is Rowena Dowell. She will be staying with us for a spell."

"Nice meetin' you, ma'am," Amos said.

He stepped outside on the porch and reached a thin, lean hand out for Rowena's handshake.

"Nice to meet you, too, Amos," Rowena said, smiling sweetly as she took his hand and shook it.

She noticed that he was dressed in black. And even though there was only a little lamplight coming from the inside of the house through the open door, his teeth were bright against his dark skin as he gave her a friendly smile.

"Like so many people, Amos lost his family in the war," Lawrence said. His smile faded. "And although slavery is no more, Amos has stayed on with me and Darren. Otherwise, he'd have nowhere else to go."

Amos took his hand from Rowena's. He turned to Lawrence. "And I'll always be grateful for yore kindness," he said in a deep, husky voice.

He turned to Rowena again. "I am shore you are feelin' the same sort of gratitude toward Massa Lawrence," he said.

"Amos, you know that I've asked you not to address me as your master," Lawrence said. He placed a gentle hand on the aging man's shoulder. "I am not your master and you don't have to keep tellin' me how grateful you are. Just like Rowena here, this is your home for as long as you wish to be a part of it."

Amos's face broke into a wide, toothy smile. "I'se so happy here," he said, his voice catching. "I just wish my Sarah could be here, too, but . . ."

He stopped and lowered his eyes.

"Now, now," Lawrence said. He placed a finger beneath Amos's chin and lifted it so that their eyes met. "Let's not dwell on the past, Amos. Let us just look forward to the future. For now, it'd be mighty fine of you to get a pot of coffee brewing for me and Rowena."

Amos smiled again, nodded, glanced quickly at Rowena, then hurried back inside the house.

"He is such a gentle, caring man," Lawrence said as he gestured with a hand toward the opened door. "He'll make your stay here as comfortable as he can. He is a treasure, Rowena. It's such a shame that he has lost so much. He doesn't deserve the ill fortune the war brought him. Nor do any of us, though, do we?"

Rowena was thrown back in time, to when she had heard the news of her father's death.

Her throat closed up the way it always did when she was reminded of how her father had died, and why.

No matter how long she lived, she would never understand why men engaged in war when it took so much from so many.

"I'll take you right on up to your room, where you can freshen up a mite before coming downstairs again to the parlor for some conversation and coffee," Lawrence said. He gestured with a hand toward the staircase. "Come. I'll show you to your room."

"That would be lovely," Rowena replied.

She climbed the stairs beside him, yet continued to look around her at the rugged surroundings.

This cabin was nothing like the mansion she had been brought up in, nor the one that Lawrence Ashton had owned.

In both homes there had been winding staircases that were lighted by great chandeliers, twinkling like diamonds from the candles burning in them. There had been large framed paintings of family members hanging on the walls, and so many other beautiful things, all of which had been destroyed by the flames of war. None of them ever be replaced.

They reached the second floor and Lawrence ushered Rowena past two closed doors. When they reached the third, he stepped away from her and opened it.

"I hope that Amos and I made it comfortable enough for you," he said. He nodded. "Go on in. I shall follow."

Rowena stepped past him and stopped just inside the room.

She was struck by the difference between this room and the rest of the house. Lawrence had gone to great lengths to make it beautiful for her arrival.

There was a huge oak four-poster bed, with a lovely, lacy canopy shadowing the beautiful bedspread that covered what looked like a plush feather mattress.

Candles were lit all around the room in wall sconces, casting dancing shadows over walls that had been papered in a soft, flowery design.

The floor was covered with a thick white braided rug. A dresser made of oak stood against the wall opposite the bed; an oval mirror reflected Rowena's image back to her.

She gasped when she saw how tired she looked and how wrinkled her dress was.

She turned to Lawrence, blushing. "I look a sight," she murmured.

"You could never look, as you call it . . . a sight," he said, chuckling.

He walked past her and placed her travel bag on a small chest that stood at the end of the bed, then reached out for her violin case.

"I remember your mother playing the violin," he said sadly as he took the case from her and gently placed it on the bed. "She always played at parties held in your home. She was quite a skilled musician."

"Yes, my mother was very talented," Rowena murmured. "She taught me everything I know."

She gazed longingly at the violin case. "Except for my memories, my violin is all that is left of my past," she murmured. "I was allowed to take it and a few clothes with me to the convent. Nothing more. Not even books that I cherished."

She went to a window and gazed out it.

Her heart seemed to skip a beat when she saw a horse corral not far from the house. The moon's glow revealed several horses inside it.

One in particular caught her attention.

It was beautiful brown animal with a white star on its forehead. She had owned a mare just like that while living in Georgia.

She swallowed back a quick urge to cry, for seeing that steed was just another reminder of all she had lost.

She had not been able to take her horse with her to the convent. Surely it had been killed or taken by the Yankees.

Lawrence moved to stand beside her. He followed her line of vision. "Ah, you're looking at my horses," he observed. "I was fortunate enough to escape with them before the Yankees came and stole them, as they stole everything else that was mine."

"Yes, I see the horses," Rowena murmured. "I see a brown one with a white star. It reminds me so much of my horse Misty. How I hated leaving that animal when I had to go live at the convent. I have no idea what happened to Misty, but I'm certain it wasn't good."

"Did you say your horse had a white star?" Lawrence asked, bringing Rowena's eyes quickly to him.

"Yes, a beautiful white star on the forehead," Rowena said, sighing.

"Was it a mare or a gelding?" Lawrence asked, searching Rowena's eyes.

Her heart raced, hoping that what she was suddenly thinking might be true. "A sweet little mare with a white stocking—"

He interrupted her. "A white stocking on her left foreleg?" he said, finishing what he was certain she'd been about to say.

Rowena placed her hands on cheeks that were suddenly hot with excitement. "Yes," she said, a sob catching in her throat. "Are you saying that you saved my horse? That the one I see tonight is . . . is . . . my Misty?"

"Yes, it must be," Lawrence said.

He was not at all surprised when she turned and ran from the room. Before he even got to the top of the staircase, she was already gone from the house.

He smiled as he followed her down the stairs and outside, to the corral.

He stood there and watched with a smile on his face, as Rowena and her horse were reunited. She stood there, in the corral, hugging the little mare.

"Misty, oh, Misty," Rowena sobbed. "How can this be? You . . . you . . . are alive and you are here, not with some horrid old Yankee!"

She wiped the tears from her eyes and turned to Lawrence.

She ran to him and flung herself into his arms, hugging him tightly. "Thank you, thank you," she sobbed. "You have no idea what you have done for me. I . . . I . . . feel as though a part of my life has been handed back to me. Oh, how I love my Misty."

She hugged Lawrence for a moment longer; then she stepped away from him. "How did you manage this?" she asked, searching his eyes. "How did you get my horse? And how did you save your own horses from the Yankees?"

"Darren, Amos, and I rounded up as many as we could when he heard the reports of the Yankee's guns in the distance," Lawrence said. "We drove the horses into the woods, and then the three of us hid among the trees until we felt that it was safe to move on. I took all the money I could carry from the safe, as well as two bags of clothes, leaving the rest to burn to ashes."

"You rescued and gave my Misty a home. Now you have done the same for me," Rowena said. She wiped renewed tears from her eyes. "How can I ever repay you? How?"

"You don't have to repay me," Lawrence said.

He again reached out and hugged her with his one arm. "It does my old heart good to make something positive happen to someone as sweet as you," he said thickly.

Suddenly Rowena grew tight inside. From the corner of her eye, she caught a sudden movement in the shadows of the trees.

She stepped away from Lawrence and peered into the woods, then gasped at what she saw.

It was an Indian on a horse.

"An . . . Indian . . ." she stammered, causing Lawrence to swing around and follow the line of her vision.

He, too, saw the Indian on horseback not far from where they were standing.

He felt like a fool for coming out in the dark without a weapon.

He had just given Rowena her world back, but now her very life might be taken away just as quickly.

"All right, redskin, you've been seen," Lawrence said, his heart racing at the thought that his own life could be over in two blinks of an eye.

After marrying an Indian woman, Lawrence had never thought he would die at the hands of one of her people.

Tall Moon saw that he had no choice but to reveal himself, although he had not planned to approach his father tonight.

His hand clutched firmly around his bow, his back tight and straight, he pressed his heels into the flanks of his steed and rode out into the open, where the moon shone its bright light directly on his face.

"Father, do you not remember me?" Tall Moon asked as he stared directly into his *ah-te*'s eyes. With difficulty he kept them there, although he was tempted to look at the beautiful, golden-haired woman.

Lawrence's face drained of color as he took a step away from Tall Moon. "Thomas?" he gasped out.

Chapter Five

Stiffening at being called Thomas, a name that he had left behind long ago when his *ah-te* had cast him from his life, Tall Moon was silent for a moment as he gazed intently into Lawrence's eyes.

No doubt his father expected many warriors to come out of the darkness of the trees behind him. Tall Moon felt a brief moment of pleasure at his father's almost palpable anxiety.

But when he glanced over at the pretty young woman and saw fear in her eyes, he knew he could not remain silent any longer. The woman was innocent of the wrongs that had been done to Tall Moon, so he should not allow her fear of him to last any longer.

He looked slowly back at his father. "No, I am not Thomas," he said. "I left that name behind when you, my father, sent me away."

Tall Moon squared his shoulders proudly. "I am now called by the name Tall Moon," he said. "My mother gave me that special name long ago when she secretly taught me the ways of my Cherokee people, while you were tending to business at the plantation."

There ensued an awkward silence, and Tall Moon saw that his words changed his father's face from pale to a deep, angry red.

Tall Moon well remembered his father's temper, and how his face could turn beet red. That sight had always set Tall Moon's heart pounding; he had felt real fear of his father during those moments.

Although his father had never laid a hand on Tall Moon, his words had often been scalding and hurtful.

He doubted, however, that his father had ever scolded Darren. It was immediately apparent after Tall Moon's mother gave birth to her second son, who so closely resembled his father, that Lawrence was filled with love for the child, love that he had never felt for Tall Moon.

It had always been there . . . the resentment, the dislike, every time his father looked at Tall Moon.

Tall Moon was not at all surprised when his *ah-te* finally chose to cast him away, as though he were worthless trash. His *ah-te* had not been able to tolerate the presence of a red-skinned son, even though his own wife had the same color skin.

"Thomas—" Lawrence began, but was quickly interrupted by Tall Moon.

"Tall Moon," he corrected stiffly. "I am called Tall Moon. That name Thomas died along with the feelings I once had for you."

He saw how those words inflamed his father even more. His *ah-te* glared back at him before speaking again.

"Well, all right, if that's the way you want to play this game, Tall Moon it is," Lawrence said, his voice drawn. "Tall Moon, when I came to this land, to decide whether or not I should establish my lumber business here, I saw in the distance an Indian village, probably the same one where I imagine you make your residence. I went no farther. I wanted no trouble from Indians. But seeing the village didn't dissuade me from establishing my business and home in this area. The cypress trees are too valuable to ignore. I just made certain to set up camp and build my home far enough from the village not to cause trouble with the Indians. I had no idea that my very own son lived in that village."

"And so you finally speak the word that you despised from the day that I was born?" Tall Moon said, smiling harshly. "You call me your son?"

"Well, I—" Lawrence began, but was again interrupted by Tall Moon.

"My people are happy here beside the beautiful White River," Tall Moon said. "I led them here far from anyone who could cause my Bird Clan trouble. So far, the white government hasn't interfered in our lives. In fact, until now, no white man has been this close to my people's homes."

"You keep calling those redskins your people as though you own them," Lawrence said, almost bitterly.

"No one owns the Bird Clan of Cherokee but the people, themselves," Tall Moon said, his hand tightening on the bow that he still held at his right side. "Although I am their chief, I do not dictate to them. It is not up to me to say what they should or should not do. As their leader, I am only there to help keep them safe . . . and happy."

All the while Tall Moon and Lawrence talked, Rowena stood quietly observing what was transpiring before her very eyes: a most unexpected father-and-son reunion, but not a happy one.

There was so much in Lawrence's attitude toward this Indian called Tall Moon that made it clear he hated claiming a man with copper skin as his son.

She was surprised by Lawrence's attitude. She sensed that behind those angry words and stares, Tall Moon was a kind man. And his appearance was so noble, so . . . so . . . yes!

So handsome!

In his buckskin attire, she could see how his muscles bulged beneath the leather.

She could see how he had acquired part of his name. He was tall, a trait that he had obviously taken from his father, for Lawrence stood over six feet.

She wondered why "Moon" was part of his name. It was intriguing, as was the man whose sculpted face and dark eyes spoke volumes as he continued staring at his father.

She so wished that she could run her hand over the smoothness of his face, where there were no traces of whiskers anywhere.

And his hair! Oh, how she loved the way his hair hung far down his back. As the evening breeze grew stronger, she could see Tall Moon's hair fluttering in the moon's glow.

She searched her memory for her earliest recollections of the Ashton family. She had lived all her life on the plantation next to theirs, so, of course, she knew both Lawrence and Darren, but had not known there was another son.

She had only known that Lawrence's wife had died while giving birth to Darren, and that she had been an Indian. Some had even said she had been an Indian princess before leaving her people to become Lawrence's wife.

Rowena's attention returned to the two men when Lawrence's voice became somewhat softer. She gazed at him in surprise as she realized that he seemed to be apologizing to Tall Moon without saying the actual words.

She watched and listened, looking from one to the other, wondering exactly where this talk was going to go. Could father and son be reunited? Could Tall Moon forgive what his father had done to him?

"You call me son now, when you want something from me?" Tall Moon said, interrupting his father once again. "Or was that a slip of the tongue?"

"Tall Moon, let me speak without interrupting me," Lawrence said. "All I want are the trees. Surely that isn't a problem, is it?"

To Tall Moon it definitely was a problem, but he felt that this wasn't the time to tell his father that he wasn't welcome to cut the majestic cypress elms in the swamp. And Tall Moon did not wish to argue in the presence of this woman. He had been very aware of the way she was looking at him, curiosity shining from her beautiful blue eyes.

Of course she had probably never been this close to an Indian before. He could not help wondering what she was thinking as she had stood there, looking at him in such a way.

He hoped that she was not afraid of Indians. Then he chided himself. He knew that he shouldn't care what she thought.

But deep inside himself, he did care, for he had to admit he was intrigued by her.

As she stood there with the moon casting its wondrous glow on her beautiful face and long, golden hair, he found it hard to concentrate on what he must say to his father.

That was why he must wait until another time to speak frankly, when she was not with them. He would be able to think more logically without her distracting him.

Since the death of his wife, which now seemed so long ago, Tall Moon had not allowed his heart to be swayed by a woman.

But this woman had definitely captured his attention. His attraction to her went deep inside himself, but he knew he must fight it with all of his being. His main purpose in life was protecting his people. He could let nothing distract him from it.

He tried not to think about her any longer, but he could not stop himself from wondering what her name was.

Surely it was as lovely as the woman who bore it.

"Tall Moon?" Lawrence said, gazing questioningly into Tall Moon's eyes.

Realizing that he had gone long without replying to his father, Tall Moon knew he should respond.

From what he remembered, his father had been a decent man in many ways. Surely he would listen to reason when Tall Moon explained why he must leave this land.

"Son . . . Thomas, oh, I mean . . . Tall Moon . . . will you come inside my house, where we can talk more comfortably?" Lawrence invited. He turned to Rowena. "And would you join us?"

Rowena was taken aback by the offer. She truly felt out of place listening to their discussion.

She smiled warmly. "I am so weary from the long trip, I truly would prefer to go to my room and bathe before going to bed," she murmured.

"If that's what you want," Lawrence said. "I'll have Amos bring you a basin of warm water and a new bar of soap."

"That would be so kind," Rowena murmured.

She then turned to Tall Moon. "My name is Rowena," she said. "It is good to make your acquaintance."

Tall Moon found himself entranced by the woman. Her voice was lilting and soft. It was like a song that whispered on a breeze through the forest on a spring morning.

"I am happy to meet you," he said, experiencing an awkwardness that he did not want to feel while in this woman's presence.

He told himself it didn't matter. Surely she would be gone soon. When Tall Moon's father moved his camp elsewhere, the woman would go with him.

He wanted so badly to ask her what she was to Lawrence. But he knew such a question would be out of place.

Rowena daintily lifted the hem of her dress and swept away.

She was soon lost from sight as she reentered the house, but she would linger much longer in Tall Moon's heart.

He was afraid that the feelings she'd aroused would remain inside him. Even if he never saw this woman again, he knew he would always remember the brief moments when they had spoken to each other, their eyes meeting, recognizing some special connection between them.

"Son, come with me," Lawrence said. He reached a hand for Tall Moon, which Tall Moon refused.

He secured his horse's reins to a tree limb, then walked beside his father toward the large log house. It was much bigger than the cabins Tall Moon was accustomed to.

In his mind's eye, he recalled the huge, white-pillared house where he had once lived with his mother and his father.

He would never forget the vast fields of cotton and the black people who worked them. He had always felt it was unfair for those people to be controlled by others. It seemed the white man saw himself as superior to anyone different from him.

Whites wanted to have everything, even the right to rule the lives of everyone else. But never again would Tall Moon allow anyone to interfere in his peoples' lives.

Right now, he would fight with words to make things right again for his people, convincing his father to move quickly away from this land. Tall Moon would always use words, whenever possible, instead of weapons.

He walked up the steps to the wide porch.

His father stepped ahead of him and opened the door. Then he stood aside so Tall Moon could enter before him.

Tall Moon went inside the dwelling and stopped abruptly. He was startled by the difference between the way his father was living now and the opulence of his other house just outside Atlanta.

It was quite evident that his father had stepped down in the world. Clearly, Lawrence Ashton was no longer a man of means, but someone who was struggling to make his way in life after so much had been taken from him.

A part of Tall Moon felt sad over his father's losses, yet another part of him felt that he deserved such a fate after all his years of ruling other people's lives.

Tall Moon could even now hear the whip as it had landed on the backs of unfortunate slaves. He had always felt blessed that his father, in his time of rage, had not used the same on him.

"Leave your weapon beside the door, if you don't mind," Lawrence said as he nodded toward the bow. "I do not allow anyone to bring firearms, or weapons of any sort, inside the house. Only Darren and I are permitted to have such things here and only because I still feel the need to protect my home. I will never get over losing the plantation in Georgia."

Tall Moon gave him a lingering, questioning look, hoping that he could trust this man who had given him life. Surely his own father would do him no harm, he thought, and leaned his bow against the wall. He also removed his quiver of arrows and rested this beside the bow.

"Come with me to my study," Lawrence said, gesturing with his one hand toward a door that led into the study.

He stopped and gazed into Tall Moon's eyes. "Do you smoke?"

"Only a pipe," Tall Moon said, recalling his father's love of cigars. "That is all. I do not smoke cigars as I know you do."

"Just how much do you remember about me and your childhood?" Lawrence asked, standing aside so that Tall Moon could enter the study.

It was a sparsely furnished room, yet there were enough chairs to sit comfortably before a crackling fire in the stone fireplace. Lawrence walked over to one and gestured with his one hand for Tall Moon to sit.

And Tall Moon did so, Lawrence sat in a chair beside him.

"I know you never liked cigar smoke, so I will refrain from smoking," Lawrence said. He stretched his long, lean legs out before him. "Now tell me, Tall Moon, all about your life after you left my home."

Tall Moon gave his father an uneasy glance. "I

would rather not," he said. "What I did after leaving your home was to begin a life quite unlike the one I had while at your plantation. It was a life I loved immediately, whereas while I lived with you—"

"Do not waste your time telling me what wrong I did," Lawrence said dryly. "What's done is done. The present is what's important, but if you don't want to talk about how things are in your life now, so be it. Let's get down to the nitty-gritty. I have come here to build myself a lumber business. Let me speak plainly. You keep your people out of my way and I'll stay out of theirs."

"You were never one to beat around the bush. I remember you explaining to me that you admired a man who got straight to the point," Tall Moon said, his spine stiffening. "And so I am the same sort of man. And because I am, I will tell you that you are not wanted here. The trees that you are felling are too valuable to this land to be taken. And your presence puts my people at risk. You must take your business elsewhere. Do you hear? You are not welcome here, as I was not welcome in your home and life all those years ago. You have entered my life again, uninvited and unwanted. I shall welcome your leaving, as you welcomed mine."

"Now you listen to me, damn it," Lawrence growled, his pulse throbbing at his temples. He leaned over to look Tall Moon square in the eye. "I have come here to begin a new life after having lost in the war, even my arm. I have invested all that I have left in this lumber operation. I can make a good profit on those trees. I won't stop harvesting them. I can't. Not after spending my last dollar purchasing everything that is needed for my lumber company."

"You can go elsewhere with that same equipment and establish your business there," Tall Moon said.

His pulse raced as the confrontation drew on. He remembered just how bullheaded his father could be. Perhaps an ultimatum was not the best approach.

Tall Moon decided to try another tactic. It was one he hated using, but it might be the only way to make his father see reason.

"Father, you owe me," Tall Moon said, standing and looking down at his father.

He stepped back as his father also rose from his chair. They were now eye-to-eye, since their heights were the same.

"You turned your back on me when I was a mere child," Tall Moon said. "Are you going to do the same now, when, as an adult, I ask something of you? Father, leave me and my people in peace. Leave us the shelter and seclusion the forest has given us."

"It is the same now as it was back then, when I sent you away," Lawrence said. He tried to hide the bitterness in his voice that he felt toward his firstborn. "You are more your mother's child than you ever could be mine, and because of that . . . I owe you nothing. Leave. Go and be with *your people*. I have a son who gives me all I need from an heir. That son is Darren."

Darren.

Tall Moon turned and looked toward the door. Then he met his father's eyes again. "Yes, you do have another son," he said harshly. "Where is he? Is he too much a coward to meet his older brother, face-to-face, eye-to-eye? Is he afraid that my Indian filth will rub off on his lily white skin?"

Abruptly, Lawrence put his hand out and placed it on Tall Moon's shoulder. In his eyes was a sudden apology. "I am wrong to have spoken to you in such a way," he said thickly. "I should never have disclaimed my firstborn. It's just that you have come into my life again at the wrong time. And as for Darren? He excused himself and left just before you arrived. He has no idea that you are here. Stay. Let you two brothers meet for the first time as adults."

Tall Moon reached up and slid his father's hand from his shoulder. "I have stayed too long as it is," he said tightly. "It is time to go."

He turned and left the room.

After securing his quiver of arrows on his back again, and picking up his bow, Tall Moon took the time to look around him again at all that was strange to him, and always would be.

He would not come again to ask for what would not be given.

He now knew that he must find another way to get his father to change his mind. If force was needed, then force it would be!

His jaw tight, he left the cabin and hurried to his horse.

He stopped suddenly when he felt eyes on him.

He turned and saw a pale face watching from an upper window of the huge cabin. By the lamp-light inside the room realized that the beautiful, golden-haired woman was standing in that window, gazing down at him. . . .

Chapter Six

Tall Moon started to mount Magic but stopped when Darren stepped out of the shadows. For the first time, ever, the two brothers' eyes met.

Tall Moon wanted to feel something for Darren, but could not find a trace of caring for him inside his heart. The man he saw was a total stranger to Tall Moon.

Flashes of memory from those days leading up to Tall Moon's banishment came to his mind. They were not happy times, for he had lost his mother during childbirth, and then he'd lost his father, too.

He was proud that he felt no jealousy of this brother who had replaced him in their father's life. It was not Darren's fault that he had been born into a world where people were not equal, not even brothers.

Darren stared tirelessly at the man he had just learned was his brother. He felt a deep resentment for Tall Moon, yet he felt a strange sort of satisfaction that their father had not shown any true affection for his firstborn when he'd come face-to-face with Tall Moon tonight.

Not so long ago, Darren had returned from his nightly ride beneath the moon, and had just started toward the corral, to leave his horse there, when he had heard Tall Moon arriving.

At the time he knew not who the Indian was, and had felt sudden fear at the possibility that this Indian might be the first of many to arrive.

He had hurriedly backed his horse into the darker shadows of the forest, his eyes searching frantically around him, wondering if more Indians were waiting to show themselves.

Were these the last moments of his life?

He had scarcely breathed when the Indian was soon discovered by Rowena. Darren's eyes had widened when he had heard the lone Indian identified as Darren's brother.

A keen resentment had filled him as he realized the Indian was his blood kin. Instead of shooting the redskin or sending him away, his father invited the savage inside the house.

Darren had remained hidden until everyone had entered the log building.

He had then gone to the corral, left his horse there, and sneaked up to the window of the house. Just inside it were his father and his brother. He had listened the confrontation between his father and Tall Moon.

He had heard enough to know that Tall Moon's arrival meant trouble.

"And what do we have here?" Darren said, breaking the silence. "What's the matter, savage? Don't you recognize your own brother?"

He laughed sarcastically. "But why should you?" he said. "Father made sure your Injun blood didn't mingle with ours. Sending you away was the best way to solve that problem."

Tall Moon's jaw tightened as he endured his brother's insults. He had wondered often just what sort of a man his younger brother had turned out to be.

Now only a few words revealed to Tall Moon a man of deep prejudice. Tall Moon knew now that this brother could never be anything to him. They had nothing in common. They were complete strangers.

They had been raised in separate ways. One was of the white world, whereas the other was of the red.

"Tall Moon, I eavesdropped on what you and Father were discussing," Darren said, breaking the awkward silence. "That's how I know who you are. My brother. A damned breed!" He laughed sarcastically. "I'm glad that I was born with our father's looks, not our savage mother's."

Those were fighting words for Tall Moon. But he would not allow himself to fall into the trap that his *a-na-da-ni-ti* was trying to set.

The insults coming from this brother cut deep into his heart, but he would not allow Darren to know this. Tall Moon was going to prove that he was a better man than Darren in all respects.

Wanting to get away from a brother who would speak such cutting words, Tall Moon quickly mounted his steed, lifted his reins, and started to ride away. Darren stepped quickly in his path, stopping him.

"I have one more thing to say to you," Darren said sneeringly. "I heard you discussing trees with Father. I know you tried to talk him out of cutting them. Listen well to what I have to say—you'd better not get in the way of me getting rich off those trees, or I'll bring the whole damn cavalry down on your dirty Cherokees. Isn't your clan supposed to be in Oklahoma with the rest of the savages, penned up on a reservation like wild animals?"

Darren glowered at Tall Moon as he continued. "Father and I don't owe you anything, so don't think you can come here and get special treatment just because you are the older brother," he snarled out. "I stood beneath the window and listened to everything you said. I heard you tell Father that he owed you because of what he did to you so long ago. Father owed you nothing then, nor does he now. And I certainly don't owe you a thing. You are not only a stranger to me, you are a damn savage!"

Tired of being called a savage over and over again by this man whom he regretted was his brother, Tall Moon stepped close to Darren and leaned into his face.

"If you cause me or my people any trouble, I, Tall Moon, will take great pleasure in scalping you," he said in a low warning. "Even though the same blood mingles inside both our bodies, you are nothing to me. Nothing!"

Tall Moon smiled and held his face close to Darren's. "And I am proud to have our mother's looks," he said tightly. "She was all goodness."

Tall Moon's threat made Darren take a quick, shaky step away. He gave his brother an uneasy look, then fled into the safety of the house.

Tall Moon mounted Magic, sank his heels into the flanks of the horse and rode away.

He smiled easily as he thought about how he had taunted Darren, threatening to scalp him. Of course, Tall Moon wouldn't scalp anyone, nor had any of his Bird Clan ever done anything as vicious as that.

But he knew that someone like his *a-na-da-ni-ti*, would actually believe the threat was real. That was all that mattered. Darren would surely think twice before causing Tall Moon's Cherokee people any trouble.

His thoughts returned to the golden-haired woman. He glanced over his shoulder at the window where he had last seen her standing. She was no longer there, but he could feel her inside his heart.

He wondered if she realized the danger she courted, a lone woman living where there were so many men, especially lumberjacks, who might have been without women for too long. During his observation of the camp, Tall Moon had seen only the golden-haired woman, no other females.

No, she surely did not know, or she would never have agreed to come and live among so many men.

Something deep inside told him that tonight

would not be the last time he would see the woman named Rowena.

He must see her again.

And . . . he would!

Ho, yes, somehow, they would know each other.

Chapter Seven

Morning had dawned. Sage was burning in the fireplace of Tall Moon's cabin to purify the air. He sat comfortably on cattail mats spread out on the floor before the fire.

He had not been out of bed for long, yet he had already taken his swim in the river, to cleanse himself for the day ahead. His long black hair was still damp as it hung down his bare back.

He was eating a breakfast of delicious corn cakes that his cousin, Sweet Sky, had made for him. As he ate by the warmth of the fire, he was lost in thought. He did not want to tell his people what he had learned, that their forest was threatened by his own father.

Tall Moon hoped to take care of the problem himself. He sighed heavily, for were it not his own *ah-te* who was responsible for this threat, he would have known just what to do.

He and his warriors would have confronted the intruders, ordering them away. And if they had not complied, they would have paid the price, perhaps with their own lives.

But these white people were brought to the White River by his own father. Worst of all, his father was in charge of the whole operation.

"Surely I can get him to listen to reason," Tall Moon said, pushing his empty wooden plate away.

Ho, surely his *ah-te* would understand that Tall Moon was only trying to protect his people. If the lumber business became a success, more whites would come to this area. Eventually, their presence would end his people's way of life here.

Ho, it had happened elsewhere. Once whites discovered something they valued in an area, they swarmed there, like bees drawn to pollen.

But the white man worked differently from bees. He ruined the goodness of everything he touched, negligent and ignorant of how things should be.

Tall Moon could not allow this to happen in the place where his people were so happy. He would make his father leave, one way or the other.

"*Ah-te*," Tall Moon whispered sarcastically to himself.

Ho, this white man was his blood kin, but he had not been a true father to Tall Moon.

While they had been talking together, Tall Moon had examined his feelings, trying to understand the conflicting emotions he felt for his father. He still yearned for the love and acceptance he'd been denied. But at the same time he felt the same resentment he had carried inside his heart since that day he had been told he had to leave his father's home, that Lawrence Ashton had decided having an Indian wife was a mistake.

Ho, Tall Moon now understood that his father

had resented Tall Moon's resemblance to his mother's people. He had come to scorn his wife because of the critical looks people gave her when his father tried to have social affairs at his huge Georgia mansion.

Tall Moon could recall how awkward his mother had been during those functions, and how those parties had tapered off, until finally there were no functions at all at his father's plantation house.

The piano that had played during the balls had grown silent, the lid closed over the keys. The house had held a terrible quietness within its walls.

It did not surprise Tall Moon that his mother had not made it through childbirth. She had dreaded giving birth to another child fathered by her white husband. The love between her and her husband had long since died. She knew Lawrence's greatest hope was that this second child would be another son, one who would resemble him and be a fitting heir.

Ho, Tall Moon had watched his mother's sadness deepen during her pregnancy. He'd seen how withdrawn she had become.

Her only pleasure was to be with Tall Moon in private, teaching him the ways of their Cherokee people. He now knew those lessons had been meant to prepare him for living among them, for she had realized that Tall Moon would be sent away, eventually.

"And, Mother, how right you were," Tall Moon said aloud, looking heavenward.

He often seemed to feel his mother's presence. Sometimes he could even feel her breath brush against his cheek, and could smell her favorite scent of roses.

Her husband had given her a bottle of rose perfume that he had brought from France after his one venture there, to trade his cotton for luxury items.

When he had returned, after a full month's stay abroad, he had sincerely seemed to have missed his family. He had brought his wife the fancy bottle of sweet-scented perfume. He had also brought Tall Moon a tiny horse carved from wood, because Lawrence knew how much his son loved horses.

Tall Moon had brought this tiny carved horse with him to his grandfather's home when he had been ordered away from the plantation. He wondered now why he had kept it

Had it been because deep down inside himself there was some love left for his *ah-te*, the father who had cast him aside as though he were trash? All he knew was that he had kept it and had stored it in a buckskin drawstring bag, among other things rarely touched by him.

The bag had since disappeared. He had no idea where it was, and he didn't care. He felt as though it had been wrong to have kept anything that was connected with a man who could disclaim his own son.

He wished that he could have brought something of his mother with him when he'd left, for there were times when he missed her so much that it was like a terrible ache deep inside him.

"Mother, are you here?" he asked, looking

slowly around him, somehow feeling her presence again, as he did so often.

Again he caught the faint scent of roses that always came when he felt her nearness. And then he seemed to feel the slight brush of something against his cheek which he imagined was the touch of her hand.

"Mother, I am so weary," Tall Moon said, swallowing hard. "*Ah-te* has entered my life again. And it is not a good way that he has come to me. He brings trouble to our Cherokee people. Guide me, lead me, Mother, in what to do. I will follow."

As quickly as the sweet aroma had come, it was gone again, but Tall Moon felt blessed to have had his mother with him, if only in this form.

As the wood crackled and popped in the fireplace, and the flames gently caressed the logs, Tall Moon stepped outside where his people were busy with their morning's activities.

Pride in his clan swelled inside his heart as he stopped and looked slowly around him. They were such a devoted, industrious people.

He knew that some women had gone into the forest to gather plants, either for healing, or for their cook pots. Among those plants would be Tall Moon's favorite, wild horehound, which he especially enjoyed eating while he was on long journeys.

Other women were on their cleared land, planting seeds that would grow into food to sustain their families along with the meat that was brought in by the hunters. When harvest time arrived, there would be plenty of vegetables in their communal garden to last the village through the long siege of winter.

In the air he could smell smoke and knew that some of the women were burning weeds by a nearby stream. They would use the ash as a salt substitute, and also in soap-making.

He could not see his warriors, but knew that many were hunting, either on land, or by canoe in the river. Both fish and game would go into the women's cook pots.

His eyes were drawn to a group of children who did not yet participate in the work of the village. When their legs grew longer and they entered their teen years, they would join his people in their various chores.

For now, they were playing games. The young braves' favorite sport was ball play. The girls were playing house with their make-believe babies made from corn husks.

All in all, everything was right in his village this morning. No one was aware of the danger lurking nearby in the swamp, where the tall trees grew beautiful and serene.

He imagined that some of his warriors might come across the lumber crews as they fished or hunted, and would bring the news to him. Wouldn't it be better to alert his people to the strangers' presence and tell them he was working on a strategy that would drive the white men away?

Among those driven off would be his father. Tall Moon realized he should have put his father out of his heart long ago, when his mother had died and his father had not allowed her body to be buried among her ancestors. Instead, he had buried her far from the mansion, without even a stone to mark her grave.

That had revealed how little she'd meant to her husband.

At first he had been blinded by her sweetness and beauty. He had not realized that it would never work for him to have an Indian wife.

Suddenly Tall Moon saw another woman in his mind's eye. The golden-haired, blue-eyed beauty, who had come to live with his father and brother.

Tall Moon had absently imagined her in his arms, even knowing how impossible it would be to take her into his life. He must always remember that such a relationship had not worked for his mother and father, two people from vastly different worlds.

Surely it would not be any different for himself if he looked for love where it should not be.

Then he had a thought that made him frown anxiously. Beautiful, tiny Rowena was living under the same roof as his brother, Darren.

He did not truly know Darren, but his attitude toward Tall Moon suggested that he was a cruel man. How would he treat Rowena?

Wearing his breechclout and moccasins, he sighed heavily and walked toward his corral, where Magic waited to be fed.

Tall Moon could not stop thinking and wondering about his brother. He was glad that Darren didn't resemble their mother, for in just the short time they had spoken, he had discovered that Darren was nothing like her at all.

Nor was he anything like Tall Moon. They were opposite in many ways besides coloring!

He stepped up to Magic. He held a hand out for the white horse, which nuzzled it, sharing a kinship that only horse and man can share.

"Magic, I am so torn over what to do," he said, now stroking his steed's withers before moving into the corral to feed him. "But there is one thing that is certain. My people come first, before the two men whose blood flows through my veins. *Ho*, I must protect my people at all cost. I must call a council to tell them of this danger."

He smiled when Magic whinnied softly, as though his steed truly understood how Tall Moon felt, and sympathized with him.

Chapter Eight

As she walked down the stairs to breakfast, Rowena felt apprehensive about her first full day at Lawrence's house.

When she reached the foot of the steps, she wasn't sure which way to go.

Earlier, Lawrence had tapped on her bedroom door to awaken her, saying that she should meet with him and the others at the dining hall. She did not know who the "others" were besides Darren. But now she could hear the hum of voices coming from the right side of the hall, where a door opened to what she concluded must be the dining room.

Rowena cleared her throat nervously and walked toward it. She stopped when Amos emerged from that room, then walked over to her. It was obvious that Lawrence had sent Amos to find her and escort her to the dining room.

"Good morning, Amos," she said, noting that he was again dressed in full black attire. The only exception this morning was a white towel draped over his right arm.

"Good mornin', ma'am," Amos said, giving her

a bright smile. "You are to come with me. Lawrence sent me to fetch you. The food is already on the table. But you must pardon everyone's manners, for no one waited for you. All of the men are already eating, except for Massa Darren and Lawrence. They should be here any minute now."

Rowena felt uneasy about entering the dining room without Lawrence, for by the sound of things, she would soon be facing a number of men, who were all strangers to her.

But she walked alongside Amos anyhow, only stopping long enough to catch her breath before going inside the dining room.

From the loudness of the voices, she guessed that those who worked for Lawrence also ate with him.

"The food is coolin', ma'am," Amos said, nodding toward the door. "Bes' you go on inside and find yoreself a place to sit down at."

Rowena nodded nervously to him, then went through the door, with Amos close behind her.

She saw from the corner of her eye that he hurried to another door that surely led to the kitchen. But Amos was soon forgotten when she saw just how many men were sitting on both sides of the long dining-room table. They were busy eating tall stacks of pancakes as Amos came back into the room, carrying even more on a huge platter.

Rowena was so taken aback by what she saw, she was momentarily too stunned to move. She knew from several references Lawrence had made last night that he ran some sort of lumber business, but she hadn't known how many men he employed.

Lordy, now she knew, for those men sitting there, crowded along the table, dressed crudely in sweat-stained shirts and soiled breeches must be Lawrence's lumberjacks. Most were thickly whiskered, and the stench of sweat permeating the room almost made her gag.

She had a notion to turn and run, for she hated even the thought of having to sit among them. She gasped and knew that her face must be flushed beet red when all of the men stopped their talking and eating and turned their eyes to her.

Some of them wore no expression at all on their faces. But there were others who leered at her, as though they hadn't seen a woman for a long time.

She felt as though she were being served on a silver platter to those men. How could her father's best friend expect her to accept this situation? Surely he knew that it was not proper to place her among so many men, with her being the only woman.

Her pulse racing, Rowena started backing up, to flee, but just at that moment Darren and Lawrence entered the room. The two men blocked her way, both looking dumbfounded at her obvious discomfort.

She shivered when she saw that Darren was leering at her as crudely as the lumberjacks.

She now knew for certain that she would never be comfortable around this man. When she had known him prior to the war, she had always felt that he mentally undressed her every time he looked at her.

She had hoped that he had grown out of that behavior, but it was obvious that he hadn't.

He was still as much of a cad as he had been when they had been growing up together on neighboring plantations in Georgia.

"Rowena, I'm sorry I wasn't here to greet you," Lawrence said. He took her gently by an elbow. "I can see how this might be a bit overwhelming to you . . . the number of men you must eat with, and all. But trust me. Everything will be all right. As you can see, the men are no longer staring at you, not when their bellies are growling for more flapjacks."

"Like mine," Darren said, chuckling as he walked ahead of them and sat down at the table. He gestured with a hand. "Bring 'em to me, Amos. And make certain you bring me plenty of that maple syrup you are so good at making."

Lawrence ushered Rowena to the table and gestured with his one hand toward a chair beside Darren.

She glanced at Darren, who gave her a strange sort of smile. She looked quickly away from him, and uneasily studied the other men. After a moment or two, she decided she'd rather sit beside Darren than the other men, who were again glancing at her as they chewed on big bites of pancake.

"I'll position you between me and Darren, so you'll feel more comfortable," Lawrence said, sliding the chair back from the table, then gesturing for her to be seated.

"Thank you," Rowena murmured, though she was far from grateful to him for placing her in such an uncomfortable position.

As she scooted the chair closer to the table, Lawrence sat down on the other side of her, sandwiching her between himself and Darren, with scarcely any room between either of their chairs.

Suddenly Lawrence backed his chair up and stood. He reached down and grabbed his empty coffee cup, then slammed it down onto the table, instantly drawing all attention his way. The men gaped at him, all the while still chewing their pancakes.

"Fellas, this here is Rowena," Lawrence said, gesturing at her, then pinning each man with his gaze. "Rowena Dowell. Her father and I were best friends before the war. We neighbored back in Georgia, each of our cotton plantations hugging the other. Feeling a need to protect our wealth, we joined the army together. We fought side by side until . . . until one day my friend took a bullet meant for me. As he lay dying, he asked a favor of me, to look after his daughter if I survived the war. Before he took his last breath I promised I'd care for sweet Rowena. And even though I was shot, too, losing my arm from the wound, I'm keeping my promise. Rowena is the same now as my daughter. Treat her accordingly, do you hear? Treat her with the same respect you would your own sister or mother. I expect nothing less from any of you. Do you understand?"

Almost in unison, the men nodded.

"Return to your flapjacks, gents, 'cause I feel a

need to put some in my own belly," Lawrence said, chuckling as he returned to his chair.

Amos came and piled Rowena's plate high with flapjacks fresh from the skillet, serving Darren and Lawrence as well.

He left the room and then came back again, bringing with him a bottle filled to the brim with syrup, which he handed to Lawrence.

Rowena stared at the pancakes. She had never seen such a huge pile in her life. At this moment, she had no stomach for even one of them, not after discovering how she'd spend all of her meals while living with Lawrence and his son.

She almost gagged at the thought. But when her own stomach let out a soft growl, she knew that she must eat, regardless of the company.

She realized that her hand was shaking when she poured syrup onto her stack of pancakes. She tried hard not to spill it, although there was no tablecloth on the scarred oak table to soil.

She knew that Darren was watching her. Ever since she had arrived in the dining room, or "hall" as Lawrence called the large room, he couldn't stop looking at her.

She had tried to ignore Darren's rudeness, but he continued to stare at her, even as he chewed on a large mouthful of pancakes, while some of the syrup rolled in a tiny stream from the corner of his mouth.

He only stopped watching her long enough to stab another bite of pancake on the tip of his fork. And then there he was, staring at her again as he chewed.

She didn't look back at him. She knew that he was probably imagining all sorts of unsavory things about her.

She sighed heavily and began eating, actually enjoying the sweet, syrup-drenched pancakes.

She smiled at Amos as he walked slowly along the table, pouring steaming hot coffee into all of the coffee cups.

Then suddenly Rowena's breath caught in her throat and her eyes widened with horror. She felt a hand on her knee under the table and knew it belonged to Darren.

She worked hard to keep her composure as she politely laid her fork down on the edge of her plate, then reached beneath the table and determinedly stabbed the back of Darren's hand with one of her long fingernails.

As Darren's eyes widened, he almost choked on the bite of pancake in his mouth. The instant he felt the pain in his hand, he snatched it away, and brought it out from beneath the table.

Rowena wanted to laugh out loud with victory when she saw that her fingernail had inflicted a long scratch on the top of his hand as he had yanked it from her knee. She smiled with pleasure when she saw small pearls of blood oozing from the scratch.

Darren glared at her as he wiped his hand clean with a napkin. She hoped he would understand her "leave me alone" look as she glared back at him.

Lawrence seemed oblivious of what had just happened. He was too busy shoving bites of pancake into his mouth, then guzzling down coffee.

Rowena heard the commotion the men made as they began leaving the table, sauntering from the room until the only people left were herself, Lawrence, and Darren.

Rowena gasped and jumped with alarm when Lawrence quickly stood up and yanked Darren from his chair with his one hand. She scarcely breathed as Lawrence pulled Darren close and glared into his eyes.

"Listen to me, son, for I won't tell you a second time." Lawrence growled out. "I waited until the men left to give you a piece of my mind about what you did a moment ago. You leave Rowena alone, do you hear? I saw what Rowena did when you began playing hanky-panky beneath the table. Damn it, son, I'll not tell you a second time—never lay another hand on Rowena or I'll take a belt after you!"

Lawrence nodded at the scratch on Darren's hand. "She should'a done worse to you than that," he said even more heatedly. "She should've grabbed you by the balls until you let her go."

Rowena blushed at Lawrence's reference to a man's private parts and stood up quickly. "Please excuse me," she said, then rushed from the room. She didn't stop until she was outside at the corral where Misty was waiting for her.

Rowena was dressed in her riding clothes, a leather skirt, long-sleeved white blouse, and knee-high leather boots. Her long hair was tied neatly with a ribbon, in a ponytail.

As soon as she had awakened this morning, she had known that she would be riding her Misty. Misty was all that remained of her past. While riding her mare she could forget her troubles for a while.

After saddling Misty, Rowena mounted her and took up the reins. She set out through the camp and before she got far, she was stunned by the activity all around her.

When she had arrived yesterday, the men had already stopped working. This morning she could see the full extent of the lumber business that Lawrence had established beside the river.

As she sat there in the saddle, her eyes wide, a raft was just arriving with a load of felled trees. She watched as these logs were wrapped with chains attached to mules and then dragged to a three-sided building where they were being made into great slabs of wood.

She sighed in relief, for she realized that while the men were busy doing their work, they did not notice she was there. She felt free to ride through the forest, for it was apparent that the men were all working nearby their camp for the time being. From the looks of things, they were working their way across the land and would eventually reach right up to Lawrence's home. If that was his plan, there would be a long empty space left on the land where the trees had once stood.

She wondered if Lawrence would then move elsewhere, to establish a new home, and continue ruining the land by removing tract after tract of trees.

It saddened her to think of such a beautiful forested land as this suddenly barren. It seemed a crime, but she knew that she could do nothing about it. It was apparent that Lawrence was a stubborn man who would not listen to reason about anything.

She recalled her father describing his friend just so. When her father had asked Lawrence not to grow his cotton so close to her father's own, his request had fallen on deaf ears. It had become difficult to know which land was owned by which man.

But knowing they had to work together when war was declared, they quickly forgot their differences and went to battle as the best of buddies.

Rowena's thoughts came back to the present when she caught a few of the lumberjacks stopping suddenly to stare at her. Recalling how she had been ogled at the breakfast table by those men, she blushed, kicked Misty, and rode away. As she entered the shadows of the forest that stretched out from the cleared land, she soon felt the same freedom that riding Misty always gave her.

She dreaded returning to the house after she was finished riding, but she had no choice except to do so. For now that was her home, whether or not she liked it. She had no money to go elsewhere, and she didn't want to return to the convent.

Her only possession of any value besides her clothes was her violin. She knew that it was worth a lot of money because it had once belonged to a well-known violinist from Paris. His name was engraved on the inside of the violin.

She couldn't pronounce it, but she knew that anyone familiar with violins would recognize it. She could get a lot of money from selling it.

But doing that would be her last resort. She adored the violin, and playing it gave her such pleasure . . . an inner peace.

She must try to find a way to accept the downside of her new life, as well as what was good about it.

She was riding now through a beautiful meadow at the edge of the forest, and could appreciate just how lovely this land was. She inhaled the sweet fragranace of spring flowers in bloom everywhere she looked, and listened to the peaceful sound of a stream as it flowed gently over pebbles and stones.

She rode onward, unaware of how far she had already gone, the noise of the lumberjacks now far behind her.

She reached up and untied the ribbon from her hair and stuffed it into her skirt pocket, then let her hair blow free in the breeze.

She closed her eyes and inhaled deeply. She envisioned herself back at her home in Georgia, riding across the land that stretched away from their large cotton fields.

"Oh, Papa, Mama, I miss you both so much," she whispered as tears sprang to her eyes. "Will I ever have a normal life again? I'm afraid I'm going to hate it here. I feel nothing but dread at the thought of returning to Lawrence's home, and all those men!"

Chapter Nine

Having decided that he had no choice but to let his Bird Clan know what was happening near their village, Tall Moon had gone from home to home to announce a council, which would include both men and women.

The children had been purposely excluded, for they did not need to have worry lying heavily on their shoulders. Instead, the young ones remained outside, playing their favorite games, oblivious of the danger that might come upon them if Tall Moon did not use his powerful leadership in the right way.

Some of his people were still filing into the large council house, their eyes looking worried; it was not a usual thing for their chief to call a council that included both men and women, and especially at this time of morning.

Councils were usually attended only by the warriors, and in the evening, after their bellies were comfortably full with their wives' delicious food.

Dressed in fringed buckskin today, his feet warm in his beaded moccasins, Tall Moon stood at the far end of the large lodge. He would wait until his people were all there and seated before speaking.

Trying to focus on anything but what he must do as soon as all of his people were crowded into the council house, Tall Moon looked slowly around him. He recalled the days that it had taken to build this place of council.

He had proudly helped, for he was filled with such satisfaction at having succeeded in bringing his people far from Georgia, where there was nothing but trouble for the Cherokee. If the white authorities had their way, they would send as many of the red men as they could to reservations.

The Cherokee had no powerful advocate in Washington to speak on their behalf as Abraham Lincoln had done for African slaves, actually freeing them. It was apparent that the white leader did not feel the same empathy for people of red skin.

This tall, whiskered, white leader in Washington had already proven that he would not fight to help Indians. It seemed that those in charge saw red-skinned people not as human beings at all, but instead, as animals.

Savages, Tall Moon thought bitterly to himself. *Ho*, that was how his proud people were referred to.

Savages!

He had to wonder if his own father and brother thought of him as a savage, too. Did it make his father's skin crawl when he thought of having to associate with Tall Moon?

Realizing that his mind had wandered, Tall Moon focused on what must be said to his people.

He watched as they filed in and spread their blankets on the oak floor, where they would sit and listen to what their leader had to say.

A warm fire burned at one end of the lodge, casting dancing shadows over the walls and sending its lazy warmth throughout the large house, which like their homes, was made of logs.

Finally they were all seated. Tall Moon was aware that everyone was watching him, waiting to see why the council had been called. He went and stood before them. He gave them a grave nod, then began speaking.

"My people, I have always chosen peace over war when possible. But today we are faced with a danger that may require fighting to defend our homes," Tall Moon began.

He saw the shock in the eyes of his people, as well as fear, and he understood.

As their leader, he had scarcely ever spoken of warring, and it pained him to have to do so now. He was glad, though, that so far he had kept them safe from the horrors of war during his times as chief of the Bird Clan.

His grandfather, who was chief before Tall Moon, had not been so fortunate. Whites had interfered in the lives of the Cherokee, causing much hardship and suffering.

When Tall Moon stepped up into the chieftainship, and he had his first council with his people, he had told them that he would try his best to see that they never had to see the bloodshed and sorrow of war again.

But now?

Would Tall Moon's *ah-te* cause all of this to change? If his father didn't listen to reason, Tall Moon would have to fight to assure the continued safety of his people.

Tall Moon wanted to reassure them that he would do everything within his power so that they could remain where they had found their happiest hours. But he was afraid some kind of violence was inevitable.

"My people, warring is the last thing I wish to bring into your lives," Tall Moon went on. "And I promise you that I will try my best to solve this problem without guns or deadly arrows."

He paused and looked slowly around, seeing dismay in his peoples' eyes.

"I will explain now what has happened that has caused me to call this early morning council," Tall Moon said. "I will tell you why it might be necessary to fight to protect what is ours."

He softly told them how he had found white men traveling down the White River on a raft that was piled high with cut trees. He explained how he had followed that raft and discovered where the trees were being taken, and what was done with them.

He hated having to tell his people that it was his own *ah-te* who had brought this lumber business to the area. But Tall Moon knew that he had no choice other than to tell them.

The Bird Clan had ignored the fact that he had a white father when they'd chosen him to take over as chief upon the death of his grandfather. He didn't want to give them a reason to regret that decision.

When he ventured on and explained his father's role in the problem, he was relieved that he didn't see resentment cloud their eyes. Instead they continued to listen attentively to all he had to say about the problem that faced them.

He sighed with relief, then said, "If my father is allowed to stay on this land, and the lumber business proves to be profitable, more and more white people will come and start their own lumber companies. Their families will join them. Soon this beautiful land will be changed forever. Whites will even kill the Cherokee in order to have the trees that now so peacefully shadow our homes."

Suddenly one of his favored warriors stood up. "If we go to war against these white tree cutters, won't that bring soldiers in to protect their people?" Red Leaf asked. "You know that is so. We could be put in a very bad position. Either way we choose to go about this, our lives will be changed, and for the worse!"

"I truly believe that my *ah-te* will not want harm to come to his oldest son," Tall Moon said as Red Leaf sat down. "A son is a son, no matter the color of his skin. Do you not do everything within your power to protect your sons?"

Everyone nodded in unison.

"I believe that after my *ah-te* has time to think deeply about this, he will understand my position," Tall Moon said tightly. "*Ho,* yes, I hope that my father will choose to do what is right for his older son."

He paused, then declared, "It is up to me to make certain that the choices my *ah-te* makes benefit the Cherokee, not the whites, for his oldest son is more Cherokee than white."

He inhaled a deep breath as he again looked from face to face. "Yet, I must tell you, if what my *ah-te* said was true, he spent the last of his money purchasing what he needed for his lumber company. If he gave it up, he would be poor . . . and if he sold it to someone else, the situation will be no better. Any white man who purchased this company from my *ah-te* would be cutting down the same trees and would, in the end, destroy our Cherokee people's way of life."

"But then what choice do we have except to go to war?" Red Leaf asked, once again standing and towering over those who sat upon the floor.

Tall Moon clasped his hands behind him. In his mind's eye he saw his mother's beautiful face, her smile radiant as it had always been when she had been with him.

Somehow he knew that she would give him a vision, show him a way to do what was right for his people, without any of them being harmed.

"I will find a way," he said, bringing his hands around to his sides. "It is my *ah-te* who has caused the problem. It is up to me to make my father see the he must leave the land of the Cherokee. There are other trees elsewhere. Surely it would not take all of his money to move to another place to fell other trees. I will pray to the Great Spirit that my father will allow us to remain in the safe haven of our home, where until now we have found such peace and happiness."

"You will make it right," Red Leaf told him, smiling. "You always do what is right. We trust you in all and everything, my chief."

That vote of confidence from his most beloved warrior made Tall Moon certain that he could make things right, not only for his people, but also his father.

"My people, this council is over," Tall Moon said softly. He watched the men and women file from the council house.

Only Red Leaf remained.

He went to Tall Moon and gave him a manly hug, then stepped back from him, smiled, and also left the council house.

Tall Moon followed.

Without taking time to return to his lodge, he mounted his horse and rode from the village.

His hair blowing in the breeze behind him, his chin held proudly high, he could feel the blessings of the Great Spirit inside his heart. He knew without a doubt that in the end, he would be victorious.

Chapter Ten

Fully enjoying this outing on her beautiful horse, Rowena had long since left the beautiful meadow behind. She had been in such deep thought about what had transpired in her life since her father's death, she hadn't paid close enough attention to where she was going.

Now she realized she was suddenly surrounded by swampy land, riding through a great cypress forest, where Spanish moss clung like veils of lace to the trees.

It was so beautiful, so serene, so absolutely lovely, yet she realized that it was also dangerous. One misstep of her horse's hooves and she could be thrown into the murky mire.

Her thoughts, even her fear of the snakes she saw coiled around some of the limbs of the trees, were forgotten when she suddenly heard a loud pecking sound.

For a moment it stopped, and then it began again more persistently.

Rowena knew right away what was making this noise: a woodpecker.

There had been many woodpeckers back home,

in the tall old live oaks that surrounded her family's mansion. She fondly remembered standing at her second-story bedroom window, watching the woodpeckers and listening to the rat-a-tat sound as it echoed into the tall, dense forest beyond the cotton fields.

She drew rein and looked slowly from tree to tree, searching for the woodpecker. With a gasp of delight, she spotted it.

She was amazed to see that it was an ivory-billed woodpecker. She had never seen this kind of woodpecker before. Those back home in Georgia had been smaller and less colorful than this one. This bird was one of the largest woodpeckers she had ever seen, almost as large as a hawk.

Not wanting to disturb the bird's intent search for food, Rowena gently tapped her heels into the sides of her horse and rode slowly onward.

She loved the towering sweetgum trees that she now began to see growing among the cypress elms. The sweetgum, too, reminded her of her outings back home, when she used to go horseback riding with her father.

Tears sprang to her eyes at these reminders of happier times. Those outings with her father had been so special.

To have him all to herself had been like magic. They had laughed together, they had talked, they had just relaxed with each other as though they had not a care in the world. Yet already war was brewing, threatening their way of life.

When they would arrive home after those long

rides, her mother would be waiting for them with a delicious meal, and then they would retire beside the large fireplace in the study.

Although the supper had been wonderful, her mother would, nevertheless, pop a huge bowl of popcorn over the flames of the fireplace. The three of them would eat popcorn and talk into the wee hours of the morning, for they all knew the danger that was coming closer to their home as the war worsened.

They had laughed and talked and eaten and pretended nothing could ever spoil those precious moments with one another.

But life wasn't meant to be that sweet for her family for very long. It seemed that a whirlwind had raged through their lives, destroying everything in its path and leaving her without either of her parents.

All that was left were memories, precious, wonderful memories.

Never a harsh word had been spoken by her father or mother. It was hard to believe that they were gone, and that she was alone in the world.

Suddenly she felt overwhelmed by loneliness, vulnerable, in a place that was so new to her, so . . .

Her breath caught in her throat when Misty, who had wandered closer to the swamp than Rowena had realized, slipped on the muddy embankment.

Rowena was thrown from the mare, landing with a loud splash in the murky water of the swamp. As she scrambled to her feet, she found she was standing waist deep in the brackish green water. For a moment, she was stunned.

Then she became keenly aware of the sound of an approaching horse.

Feeling desperate to get back on Misty so she could ride away from whoever was there with her in the forest, she tried to scramble to her feet. But she kept slipping and sliding back into the water.

Suddenly she lost her balance and fell over, face-first, onto the muddy embankment. When she finally got her footing and was standing, for the moment she couldn't see through the mud on her eyes.

But she did hear a voice . . . a very masculine voice telling her that she would be all right.

And then she felt strong hands lifting her bodily from the water. As she was taken to stand on dry ground, she used her fists to clear her eyes.

When she was finally able to see, she was stunned to see who had rescued her.

It was the same Indian that she had seen last night. She had heard his name spoken. It was intriguing, just as intriguing as the Indian himself.

Tall Moon.

Yes, his name was Tall Moon.

As his midnight-dark eyes gazed steadily into hers, Rowena's knees almost buckled beneath her.

Once again, she marveled at his long black hair, which fell far down his back, as well as his sculpted features.

And how could she not be very aware of the muscles bulging beneath his buckskin attire?

All of this she noticed in only a matter of minutes. But then it dawned on her that she should be afraid of this man since he was an Indian.

Yes, she did recall his noble handsomeness from last night, but she also remembered the angry threat she'd overheard from her window when Darren had talked with the Indian. Tall Moon's words even now turned Rowena's blood cold.

He had threatened to scalp Darren!

Although Tall Moon was stunned to have come across the woman who so intrigued him nearby his people's village, he could hardly keep himself from laughing at the sight of her. She was standing there covered with mud, and the brown mess hid her loveliness.

Now that she had her eyes wiped clean, he saw in her lovely blue gaze a mixture of emotions. The most prominent one was fear.

"Do not be afraid," he softly encouraged. "I am an *i-ga-na-le-i*. That word in my language means friend. I offer you friendship. I would never harm you. I am *ani-yun-wiya*, Cherokee, of the *Ani-dji-skwa*, the Bird Clan. That name was chosen for our clan because of my people's fondness for birds. I am chief of the Bird Clan."

"How can you say that you are my friend, when . . . when . . . you are an enemy to Darren Ashton?" she found the courage to ask.

She was more intrigued now than ever to know that she was in the presence of a powerful chief.

"Last night I heard you threaten Darren," she quickly added. "You . . . said . . . you would scalp him."

Tall Moon couldn't help himself this time . . . he did laugh, then went somber when he placed his hands on her shoulders. He was saddened when his action made her wince, no doubt from fear.

Yet he was aware of something else . . . she did not step away from him.

"I have never scalped and never will," he said thickly. "I just used that as a ploy to put the brother I have never known in his place. My brother, Darren, made threats to me that he should not have spoken."

"Yes, I know. I was watching you and Darren together last night, from the upstairs bedroom window where I stood," she said. She was beginning to feel more at ease with him, but felt acutely aware of his hands on her shoulders as the warmth bled from them through the wetness of her blouse into her own flesh. "How is it that one brother is white and the other is—"

"Of red skin?" Tall Moon supplied, gently interrupting her.

He slowly took his hands away from her shoulders, very aware of her sighing as though with relief after he did so.

"My father, who is white, married a Cherokee Indian princess," he said. "His Cherokee wife bore him two sons. One son was born with her coloring, the other in the image of his father. The one with her skin color was sent away when she brought into the world a son who resembled his father. The son who was sent away was Tall Moon. The other, the one who was allowed to stay, was Darren. . . ."

Seeing that the woman had begun to tremble

with cold, he thought that enough time had been spent in idle talk. He wanted to get her where she could be made more comfortable.

"I will tell you more later if you wish to hear it," Tall Moon said. He looked into her eyes again. "We are closer to my village than my father's home. Let me take you to my lodge, where you can cleanse yourself of the mud. Then I will see that you have dry, clean clothes."

He paused, then asked, "You were not harmed by the fall? If you were, I can take you to my shaman once we enter my village."

"It is only my pride that is wounded," Rowena said, blushing. "Can your shaman help such a thing as injured pride?"

He smiled good-naturedly. "No, I do not think so," he replied.

Hearing the gentleness in his voice, and seeing kindness in his eyes, Rowena no longer felt even a trace of fear at being alone with him.

Surely she could trust him to do only as he suggested, nothing more. She realized she wanted to seize this very rare opportunity to see an Indian village firsthand. And she also wanted to be with this man. He truly intrigued her, especially now that she didn't see him as a threat.

"That would be so kind," she murmured, hardly able now to stop trembling from the cold swamp water.

Seeing Misty standing dutifully on the bank, Rowena went to the mare. Her breath caught in her throat when Tall Moon joined her, quickly helping her into her saddle.

The longer she was with him, the more evident his kindness was toward her.

And ah, his noble handsomeness! She could not help being deeply attracted to him.

She smiled awkwardly down at Tall Moon from her saddle, then watched him go to his own horse, a beautiful white stallion. As soon as he had mounted, she rode off on her own steed beside him.

"Your horse is beautiful," she suddenly blurted out, bringing Tall Moon's eyes back to her.

"My horse has a name. I call him Magic," he said, his eyes now roaming over her mare. "And yours? What is the name you gave your beautiful steed?"

"Misty," she murmured, still rejoicing that Lawrence had rescued her mare, and then given it back to Rowena. "Misty has been mine since I was just a girl."

"How is it that you have this horse with you, when I did not see it arrive at the same time you did?" he asked, recalling the first time he had seen her and how he had instantly been intrigued by her.

"You . . . saw . . . my arrival?" she asked, searching his eyes. "I . . . did not see you."

"I was not where anyone could see me," he said, his voice drawn. "I was not there by invitation. I was drawn to the lumber camp when I saw that trees were being cut down close to my people's home. And when I followed to where the felled trees were taken, I discovered that the man who was responsible for the destruction was my very own blood kin . . . my father."

"How long had it been since you had last seen him?" she asked, hoping she wasn't asking a question he would not wish to answer. She had always been too open about things, too "nosy," as her father had teasingly put it.

"It is something I would rather not discuss," Tall Moon said thickly. "Not now, anyhow."

"I'm sorry if I asked something too personal," Rowena said, blushing. "I am sometimes too inquisitive."

"It is good to want to know things," Tall Moon replied, slowly smiling at her. "But sometimes it is best not to want to know too much too soon."

"I apologize," she murmured, blushing beneath the drying mud on her face. "You asked about Misty and how I have her with me. I lost almost everything during the war, but Lawrence saved Misty when the soldiers attacked our neighboring plantations. When I saw Misty among his other horses last night, it was like magic that she would be there. I will forever be grateful to Lawrence for having saved my horse."

"I am happy for you," Tall Moon said. "But how is it that you have come to Arkansas to live with my father and brother?"

"Lawrence Ashton was my father's best friend. When my father took a bullet meant for Lawrence, he asked his friend to care for me," she explained. "Your father promised he would give me a home."

Silence fell between them as Tall Moon again looked straight ahead and rode onward. Rowena, too, fell into her own awkward silence as she rode alongside him.

He was the one to break the silence between them as he glanced over at her. "I must convince my father to abandon his plans to cut trees so close to my peoples' village," he said. "It is because of my Cherokee people that I am asking this of him. The presence of white men is a threat to my people's way of life. When white men interfere with the Cherokee, no good ever comes of it."

"Did you speak to your father about this?" Rowena asked, gazing into his dark, hauntingly beautiful eyes.

"Yes, I told him," Tall Moon said. "But he closed his ears to the truth, just as he closed his eyes when his son was born in his wife's image instead of his own, those long years ago. My father is not a reasonable man. He is not someone who wishes to see the truth. He will never admit the wrong he is doing, for too much money is involved."

"Surely if you talk to him again, he will listen to reason," Rowena murmured, but then she had another thought. "On the other hand, there is Darren, who does not seem the sort to be dissuaded easily, even if you should persuade your father that what he is doing is wrong."

"Sometimes words are not enough," Tall Moon said tightly.

Chapter Eleven

The sun was almost at the midpoint in the sky. It was time for the lumberjacks to stop their work and come into the dining hall for their noon meal.

Lawrence was in his office, at his desk, while Darren sat opposite him in an overstuffed chair.

They were supposed to be reviewing their recent expenses, but Lawrence couldn't get Rowena off his mind.

He had expected her home by now, and wondered if she might be purposely delaying her return so that she wouldn't have to eat with the lumberjacks again. He had realized immediately this morning how uncomfortable eating with the men made her.

He had thought about her reaction and had wondered if he should allow her to eat elsewhere. Ultimately, he had decided not to make special arrangements for her. He had accepted her into his life because of a promise to his friend, but that didn't mean that she must be treated like a shrinking violet.

She would have to get used to living there, among all of the men. With so much work being done from morning until night, he could not let her get in the way of progress, for time was money.

"Father, your mind and your eyes have strayed again from business," Darren suddenly said, his eyebrows lifted. "What's going on? Is it my brother? Or . . . is it something else?"

Lawrence cleared his throat nervously as he turned his attention to Darren. "No, it has nothing to do with your brother," he said thickly. "It's Rowena. She's been gone for way too long. I can't help worrying about her out there. Do you think she's lost in the swamp? Could she have gone that far? Or could one of the lumberjacks have seen her leave and followed her? You know how most of them looked at her. There was hunger in their eyes this morning at the breakfast table, and it was not for flapjacks. They've been without women for too long. And Rowena is . . . such a pretty little thing. Perhaps one of the men could not ignore the temptation."

He kneaded his brow and shook his head slowly back and forth. "Surely not," he growled. "Not if he values his life. If anyone lays a hand on that sweet thing, he'll have hell to pay."

He glowered at Darren. "And, son, that includes you," he said dryly. "That little trick you played at breakfast was damn foolish. Did you truly believe she'd allow you to touch her under the table?"

"I've already apologized for that," Darren said, squirming uneasily in his chair. "So I wish you'd just forget about it. There's much more to think about, Father, than the mistake I made by trying to get a feel of that pretty little knee."

"I'll forget about it when I know you'll not do anything as asinine again," Lawrence said, squinting his eyes angrily as he gazed directly a Darren. "Now back to the problem at hand. Perhaps it wasn't all that wise, after all, bringing Rowena here, among so many men, where she's the only female. But I promised her father that I'd watch over her and keep her safe. I don't go back on my promises, especially to a man who saved my life by giving up his own."

"No matter what you promised, you know that having Rowena will cause only trouble," Darren said. "Maybe you can give her enough money to help her get settled elsewhere."

Lawrence leaned forward, his eyes narrowing as he was filled with disappointment and resentment toward a son who had disappointed him too often.

"Do you mean . . . pay her off . . . as though she's a worthless wench?" he growled. "That isn't what her father had in mind when he asked me to look after her. So know this, son, I'll never do anything that could bring harm to Rowena. Sending her out there in a world gone crazy from that damnable war would be the worst thing I could do for the sweet thing."

Darren chuckled. He smugly crossed his legs at his ankles and slowly ran his hands up and down the arms of the chair as he smiled crookedly at his father. "Father, if you are worried so much about the little gal, why don't you marry her? That'd sure take care of all of her problems, wouldn't you say?"

Finding that suggestion highly offensive, Lawrence turned bright red. He slammed his fist on his desk. "Shut your mouth," he ground out. "You know I'm too old to marry her. And that certainly wasn't what her father had in mind when he asked for my help."

"Well, I can't lie when I say that bedding down with Rowena has come to *my* mind," Darren said, his eyes gleaming with the thought of having the little beauty's warm body lying next to his.

He could already feel the softness of her pure white shin. He could not help the stirring in his loins when he went further in his imagination about what he'd do to her.

"What's that you said?" Lawrence demanded, raising his eyebrows. "Surely I heard you wrong."

"No, not at all," Darren said. "I'm only human, Father. Just like the rest of the men who work for you, it's been too long since I've had a woman. Surely all of the other men who got a whiff of her perfumed body were feeling the same hankering for her."

His eyes danced as he smiled slowly at his father. "Admit it, Father," he said in a tone of voice that sent a cold shiver up and down Lawrence's spine. "You've had longings of your own, haven't you? Wouldn't Rowena feel mighty good lyin' next to you in your bed?"

Instantly enraged at the insinuation, at his son's arrogant refusal to heed Lawrence's earlier warning, Lawrence leapt from his chair so quickly, it fell over and landed on its back on the floor.

He rushed around the desk and slapped Darren

on the face. "Get out of here," he stormed. "Go and do something useful instead of spending your time saying nasty, worthless things. Our business discussion seems to have gotten lost in the filthy mire of your imagination."

His face stinging and hot from the blow, Darren was so stunned by what his father had done, he just sat there for a moment, staring up and into his father's angry eyes.

"Did you hear me?" Lawrence shouted. He pointed to the door. "Get out of here, and for a change, make yourself useful."

Red-faced, and now so angry at his father he could taste the bitterness of bile in his mouth, Darren glowered at Lawrence. Then he rushed from the chair and stomped from the room.

Once outside, he turned and glared at the office window. His father was standing there, looking past Darren toward the swampy area of the forest.

His father was probably worrying about Rowena again. Why did he seem to care more about her than about his own son? Did he care at all how humiliated Darren was, to have a father show such obvious hatred for him?

That made Darren think of someone else.

His brother who now went by the name Tall Moon.

He was afraid that his father would soften toward this son whom he had cast away so long ago. Perhaps Lawrence felt guilty for having done such a thing.

Darren feared his father might replace him with

Tall Moon. Was it possible he would now choose to cast his second-born aside?

It did seem that his father's ire toward him had worsened since Tall Moon's arrival.

"I can't allow that to happen," Darren whispered to himself as he stroked his throbbing cheek, which still held the imprint of his father's hand on it.

Darren would make his father pay for striking him.

"You will be sorry," he whispered as he walked toward the lumber mill with a twisted grin on his face. "I will find a way to make you pay . . . and pay with your life, if that is what it takes to keep you from making a fool of me."

"Hey there, Darren!" shouted Sam, one of the lumberjacks, as he saw Darren walking toward him.

Sam's eyebrows lifted when he saw how red Darren's cheek was. He suspected Lawrence Ashton was to blame, for it was obvious that Darren's father had little use for him.

Sam chuckled as he looked more closely at the handprint.

"Hey, Darren, did you walk into a door?" he taunted.

"Just shut up," Darren mumbled.

He walked angrily past Sam. It was more obvious each day that the men saw the animosity between father and son. It was becoming impossible to hide.

His father had pushed him into a corner, giving him no choice but to end this battle of wills.

And he planned to carry out his plan one day soon, very, very soon.

Yes, he knew just where and how it would happen.

He glanced down at the river, where several logs floated, almost locked together. Logs were regularly left in this bend of the river before being taken to the mill for cutting.

Yes, that was how he'd do it.

He could see the "accident" now, how his father would plead with him, and how good it would feel to ignore him!

Chapter Twelve

Rowena had never been in an Indian village before, but she had seen pictures of them, and so she'd expected to see tepees. She was stunned as she rode into Tall Moon's village with him, and saw cabins, instead.

And not only that. She saw pens of sheep, chickens, hogs, and cattle, as well as a large corral of horses.

Beyond the village of log cabins was a garden just being prepared by women, who were hoeing and planting various seeds. She saw other women sitting outside their cabins, at spinning wheels, spinning wool from the sheep in a pen near the horse corral.

She was very aware that almost everyone had turned to look at her.

Even several children at play stopped and stared, huddled together as though frightened by this strange woman their chief had brought among them.

Rowena wondered why they were so afraid of white people when their own chief had white blood running through his veins.

Or was it her? Was it because she was so strange looking with the mud plastered on her clothes as well as her face?

She could smell the stench of her own body and clothes. She knew she must be a sight.

She hadn't eaten for a while and was now very aware of the rich smell of roasting meat and corn coming from some of the cabins. The smell was so delicious, she heard the rumble of her stomach as it noisily growled.

Tall Moon had seen everyone's reaction to Rowena as well. "You are the first person with white skin who has been allowed to visit my Bird Clan since I led them safely here," he said, drawing Rowena's eyes to him.

She edged her horse closer to his, feeling safer beside him.

"Many of the Cherokee people were seized by the white cavalry and herded like animals into holding pens until they were taken to live on reservations," Tall Moon continued. "When those Cherokee people were forced from their homes, many fled in different directions. My Bird Clan was among the refugees who successfully eluded the white government. When my people see white skin, they can only believe they see an enemy."

"I had no idea such a terrible thing had happened," Rowena said softly, her spine stiff as she again looked slowly around her. She felt as if the gazes of these people were burning into her flesh. "Surely I am not welcome here. Perhaps I ... should ... go."

"You are here because I brought you," Tall Moon

said, drawing rein. Rowena did the same, for she did not want to get any distance away from him and his protection.

Tall Moon looked around him, at those who stood staring and frowning. "My people, this woman is our *un-a-liy*, our friend," he said. "Her name is Rowena. I told her that I was bringing her to a place of friends, so return to your chores. This woman was in trouble. I offered her help."

He motioned with a nod of his head toward Rowena. "As you can see, she wears the trouble all over her," he said, smiling and hoping that his joke would lighten everyone's mood.

A number of people smiled in response and they all went back to what they were doing before he and Rowena had arrived.

"*O-ge-ye*, come. Come with me to my home," Tall Moon said, smiling at Rowena. "My people understand now. Some might not approve, but they understand their chief would never pass by anyone who is in trouble, especially a helpless woman, white skinned or not."

"I felt their coolness toward me," Rowena said, flicking her reins and riding alongside Tall Moon again. "Perhaps this was not a good idea at all. Perhaps I should leave."

"Look around you," Tall Moon encouraged. "Do you not see that all of my people now are tending to their chores? Even the children have returned to their play. They all know that if their chief sees you as no threat, then you are no threat."

"Thank goodness," Rowena said, reaching a

hand to her chin when the dried mud on it began to itch.

To get her mind off the sensation, she looked again at the spinning wheels and the women making yarn with them. "I am so amazed at seeing the spinning wheels in your village," she commented.

"Sometime ago, as we were searching for a place to call home, our clan came upon a people from another country, called Ireland," Tall Moon explained as he drew up in front of his cabin.

Rowena gazed curiously at it, noticing that it was much larger than the others in the village.

"These were kind people," Tall Moon continued. "They showed the women of our Bird Clan how to use spinning wheels, even traded them to us, as well as sheep, for warm blankets that attracted them with their bright colors. Since then, the women of our Bird Clan make our winter clothes out of sheep's wool. These people also gave my people seeds of many foods to plant, among them Irish potatoes. It was a good trade, do you not agree?"

"Yes, a wonderful trade," Rowena said, dismounting from Misty as Tall Moon swung himself off Magic. She stood there, still gazing at the large cabin. "And this is your home?"

"*Ho*, my home," Tall Moon said, gesturing with a hand toward the door. "Come inside. I will leave only as long as it takes for me to go to my cousin Sweet Sky, who will then carry you water to bathe with. When I return I will bring you a dress."

"I doubt that my clothes will ever be worth anything again," Rowena said, laughing softly as she gazed down at her mud-stiffened skirt. Her boots had shrunk on her feet, and felt so tight now her toes ached.

"I doubt they will, either," Tall Moon said, laughing good-naturedly. "Come inside. I want you to feel comfortable in my home. There is no woman there, for I do not have a wife, but my home is as I want it to be."

When he said that he had no wife, Rowena felt a rush of gladness. She didn't know why his words should please her so much, yet . . . yes, she *did* know. She was more attracted to this man by the minute, and each time he talked, his deep, resonant voice seemed to reach inside her heart. She knew that she was becoming enthralled by him, and knew that she shouldn't.

Judging by the way his people had reacted to her presence, she knew that they would only tolerate her for a short time, and then she must leave.

But first she would clean off this annoying mud. She realized how awkwardly she was walking because of the mud that had dried on her boots, and knew that Tall Moon had seen, too.

She could hardly wait to get out of her dirty clothes. She knew that she would burn them at her first opportunity.

But she had to wonder what sort of clothes she would be wearing when she returned to Lawrence's home. Would it be a lovely Indian dress?

She smiled at the thought. She knew that would surely rile him since he disliked anything that had to do with Indians, even though his own son was an Indian.

Although she was grateful to Lawrence for having taken her in, she was disturbed by the way he had treated Tall Moon, for this was a man who seemed good, through and through.

Any man who would help a stranger as he had helped her was a man of good heart and deserved to be treated with respect, especially by his own father.

Rowena stepped inside the cabin after Tall Moon, and was impressed by how clean it was. And she loved how it smelled of sage and cedar. It was a good combination of aromas that made the cabin smell fresh and wholesome.

His house was so clean, she felt that she shouldn't soil it with her muddy shoes and clothes. She stopped just inside the doorway and waited for him to suggest what she must do.

She noticed how sparsely furnished his cabin was. In this outer room were a few storage chests, some simply made wooden chairs, and a table. Candles burned in candleholders on the table.

At the far end of the room was a tall stone fireplace, with several mats on the floor before the hearth.

She turned quickly to Tall Moon. "I am still surprised that you and your people live in cabins and not tepees," she blurted out.

"My ancestors, not so long ago, lived in tepees, but this generation of Cherokee prefers otherwise," Tall Moon said. He went and placed a log on the fire, and soon great flames were shooting upward into the chimney.

He turned back toward Rowena, gesturing with

a hand for her to come on to nearer. "The men build dwellings. The women make what has been built a home."

He chuckled as he gestured with a hand around him. "My home lacks a woman's touch, do you not think so?" he asked, his eyes moving slowly back to her.

Rowena blushed. "I think it is just fine," she said softly.

She then quickly added, "It's hard to understand why the white authorities can't see how industrious a people you are. I sense that all you want out of life is to be left alone, to be able to live in peace."

"And so you understand more about us than I thought," Tall Moon said. He went to her. He wanted so badly to put a hand on her cheek, yet the mud kept him from touching her. "Go and sit before the fire on the mats. I will leave now. Soon you will have water, and then clean clothes. I will return later."

"Thank you," Rowena murmured. She followed him to the door, then closed it after him and walked over to stand before the fire, but stepped quickly away from it. The heat of the flames caused the mud on her face to feel even more uncomfortable.

"Drat it," she murmured.

She was longing to wash, but she must be patient. Surely in a matter of minutes . . .

The door slowly opened.

Rowena turned and saw a pretty, young woman coming into the cabin. She was carrying a basin of water and a towel was draped over her right shoulder.

As the pretty maiden stepped up to her, Rowena could see a bar of soap floating in the water, and also a cloth at the bottom of the basin.

"Tall Moon asked me to bring these to you," Sweet Sky said, and Rowena was struck by the sweetness of her voice.

Rowena noticed how slender yet shapely the maiden was in her beaded doeskin dress, which clung to her curves. She wore knee-high moccasins, that had been beautifully beaded.

Her coal black hair was worn in one long braid down her back. Her copper face was round, making her dark eyes seem even wider than they truly were.

Long black lashes shaded her eyes, and when she smiled, Rowena saw a deep dimple on her right cheek.

Jealousy surged through Rowena. She was certain that Tall Moon enjoyed this woman's company very much. She was exquisitely pretty.

But Rowena reminded herself that the lovely woman was his cousin, nothing more.

"I speak your language well," Sweet Sky murmured, smiling and deepening her dimple. "I know your name. I find it enchanting. My chieftain cousin said you are called Rowena."

"Yes, my name is Rowena," Rowena murmured as she accepted the basin of water from Sweet Sky. "And I know your name. Tall Moon said that you are called by the name Sweet Sky."

"That is the name given to me by my mother,"

Sweet Sky said, smiling and nodding. "My *ah-te* quickly approved, for he approves of everything my mother says or does. He is very much in love with her."

"That word *ah-te*," Rowena said, an eyebrow arching. "What does it mean?"

"That is the Cherokee word meaning father," Sweet Sky murmured. Her eyes moved slowly over Rowena, then she smiled again. "I will leave you to your bath."

"Yes, I do not smell or look very pleasant," Rowena said, laughing softly.

"We will talk later," Sweet Sky said, then left Rowena with the basin of water.

But Sweet Sky came in again before Rowena even had a chance to place the basin on the table.

This time she was carrying a beautifully beaded buckskin dress draped from arm to arm. Resting on this stretch of dress was a pair of beautiful moccasins, with beadwork matching that on the dress.

"Tall Moon sent these for you," Sweet Sky said, taking the dress and moccasins and placing them on one of the chairs. "We Cherokee wear clothes made from animals as well as some made from sheep's wool. Today you will be wearing a dress and moccasins made from deer skin."

With that, Sweet Sky departed, leaving Rowena to finally wash off the mud and stench that permeated the room.

Without hesitation, Rowena slipped out of her clothes, then after quite a struggle, finally got off her boots.

She eyed them sadly, for she knew that she could

never wear them again. She had worn these very boots while living home, when both her mother and father were alive and happy.

"Slowly everything has been taken from me because of that damnable war," Rowena murmured, then sighed blissfully when she sank her hands into the warm basin of water and brought a handful to her face.

Oh, Lord, nothing had ever felt as good as that water removing the tight mud from her face.

She continued washing until her body was sparkling clean and smelling of roses from the bar of soap that she had used. Then she immersed her golden hair in the water and scrubbed her scalp, rubbing the soap onto her hair over and over again until she knew that it must be clean.

After rinsing it the best she could in the sudsy water, she grabbed the towel and used it to fluff her hair as dry as possible.

When all of this was done, and her hair shone again, Rowena slipped into the beautiful beaded dress and matching moccasins, then went and sat before the fire on the mats.

She sat there, combing her hair as best she could with her fingers as she gazed into the fire.

Every time she heard footsteps outside the cabin, she looked quickly toward the door. She was disappointed each time when those footsteps went onward and it wasn't Tall Moon.

She wanted to be with him again. Her racing heart was proof enough of that.

Chapter Thirteen

While the logging work was at its busiest, with new raft loads of logs coming in every time Darren looked toward the river, he decided to take this opportunity to sneak away.

He and his best buddy, Lloyd Arden, wanted to go to a special spot in the woods, where there was going to be some hot excitement tonight after the evening meal was over.

After seeing that his father was too busy giving orders to miss him for a short while, Darren looked over at Lloyd. One nod to his friend and Lloyd sneaked away into the dark shadows of the forest. Moments later, Darren ran and joined him there. Together, they hurried to their horses, which they had tied in the woods earlier.

"We don't have long," Darren said, mounting his steed while Lloyd did the same. "Hurry, Lloyd. It's best that we get as far away as possible before my father realizes we are gone."

The new leaves of the huge elms and poplar trees were bright green in an occasional beam of sunshine that worked its way through the thick foliage overhead.

"Darren, one of these days your father is going to realize what we're doing, and when he does, all hell will break loose," Lloyd said, wiping pearls of sweat from his brow with the back of a hand.

His breeches and red plaid shirt were sweat-stained; his face was clean-shaven.

His blue eyes were penetrating against his sun-tanned face; his blond hair was worn clean and neat to his shoulders.

"What are you going to do then, Darren, when your father finds out what you are promoting here in the forest so close to his home?" Lloyd demanded.

"It's my home, too, damn it," Darren growled out as he gave Lloyd a deep frown. "And one day soon it'll all be mine, so stop frettin' so much."

"What do you mean . . . one day soon it'll all be yours?" Lloyd asked, raising an eyebrow. "What are you planning to do to your father, kill him?"

Darren went quiet and looked quickly over his shoulder to be sure that his father wasn't nearby. He was relieved when he saw no sign of him. He did not want his father to hear Lloyd's comment or to learn what Darren was involved in besides the lumber business.

Cockfighting.

Darren had established his cockfight arena far from where the trees were being felled, so that his father would not discover it.

His father rarely traveled away from his home. Lawrence rarely even went into town, because his skill at riding a horse had been hampered by the loss of his arm.

When his father tried to sit in the saddle, he lost his balance. Afraid he might truly fall from the horse, he just never tried anymore. Everyone else did the work that required riding horses.

Darren's father only gave the orders and Darren resented how good he was at doing it.

But Darren resented almost everything his father did these days. In fact, he had no love, whatsoever, for the man. And the feeling was mutual.

Darren was sure his father would disapprove of his cockfighting. He had seven well-trained cocks and took bets from the men who worked for him and his father, to see whose roosters would be victorious . . . Darren's or Lloyd's.

Finally he and Lloyd reached the cleared area where a cabin had been built to house the roosters. This was where Darren escaped when his father either worked on his journals or retired early.

Darren smiled to himself as he thought about his father not being interested in Darren's pastimes after working hours.

Darren had many an hour to indulge himself without worrying about being caught.

"Seems nothing has bothered the roosters," Darren said, dismounting his horse. He secured its reins, then opened the gate in the fence around the clearing. "Everything seems hunky-dory. Let's go and see if the roosters seem primed for the kill. You know that tonight one of either yours or mine will bite the dust."

"Yours for sure," Lloyd said, also dismounting and securing his horse's reins to a low tree limb.

He chuckled as he went inside the fence with Darren, closing the gate behind them.

"Don't be so sure about that," Darren said, walking toward the cabin where the roosters were housed. "I'm very careful about the cocks I raise for these contests."

He opened the door of the cabin, the stench of filth making his nostrils flare.

He gave Lloyd a sly grin. "Just look at mine, Lloyd," he bragged. "Take a very good look. Tell me now that your roosters are better than mine."

Lloyd stepped up to the cages that housed his own roosters. He smiled at what good shape they were in.

He knew they were ready to be released from their small cages. They would be ready to attack the others just out of anger at having been penned-up in such tiny quarters for so long.

As a cock owner, he was proud of how power-ful his animals were. He trained them whenever he had time away from his work. He came to the cabin and made sure that his roosters were ready for the moment when they would be made to face another one.

Darren squatted down low before his cages. He smiled at one rooster in particular. "Seems you're ready to bite off the head of your opponent, aren't you?" he said, laughing loudly. "Just look at you. Aren't you a pretty one? My pride and joy."

His gaze lingered on the rooster. It was a good fighting cock, that was for sure.

Its head was small. Its eyes were lit with fire. Its neck was strong.

"It's good that your roosters and mine get plenty of time to observe one another from their separate cages, testing each other ahead of time, but only with heated glares," Darren said, chuckling. "Believe me, Lloyd, both yours and mine are ready for the challenge."

He reached inside a bag of seed and grabbed a handful, then dropped it inside the cage. He watched how the rooster quickly ate it.

"Hungry, eh?" Darren said, laughing at how hungry the rooster was. Hunger made his cocks even meaner!

He stood and looked over at Lloyd's cocks. He knew that they were as mean as they came.

"Lloyd, you've done a fine job getting your cocks ready for the fight," Darren said, rising and going to kneel beside Lloyd as his friend gazed at his prized cocks.

"Yeah, they're mighty fine, if I do say so myself," Lloyd bragged. He smiled smugly at Darren. "We'll soon see who has done the best job of preparin' for the duel tonight."

"Lloyd, you can try and fool yourself all you want, but you have to know by looking at my cocks that nothing compares with them," Darren said, chuckling. "Not even yours, my friend. Not even yours."

"Won't be long now and we'll see who can brag loudest," Lloyd replied, laughing. "My friend, there won't be nothing for you to brag about and you know it."

Trying not to get angry at Lloyd, who seemed too smug for his own good, Darren stood up and placed his fists on his hips. "Soon all hell will break loose when we pit these sons of a gun against each other," he said. "Then we'll see whose cock is the best."

He started toward the door. He'd had as much of the stench in the cabin as he could stand, as well as the nonsense his friend was feeding him.

He hurriedly opened the door, but stopped before leaving.

He turned and gave Lloyd a crooked smile. "May the best cock win," he said, laughing hard as he strode through the fenced-off area. Lloyd soon joined him, and they rode their horses back to camp.

"This cockfighting is in my blood," Lloyd said, his blue eyes sparkling with eagerness to see the cocks pitted against each other. "There just isn't anything like watching two cocks fight each other to the death. It kind of reminds me of the way the Injuns battle the cavalry. They don't give up easily even though they know they are outnumbered."

Darren looked quickly over at Lloyd, wondering if his friend could have been nearby when Darren's brother had been mouthing off last night. Had Lloyd heard anything?

Did he know that Darren had an Injun for a brother?

His eyes narrowed angrily with disgust at the thought of having to put up with such embarrassment. He would do whatever was necessary to prevent the lumberjacks from learning the truth about Darren's family.

Chapter Fourteen

Rowena turned, then anxiously rose to her feet when she heard the door to Tall Moon's cabin open. She had been anxiously anticipating Tall Moon's return.

He stepped into the cabin carrying a tray of food, which made Rowena's stomach react to the delicious smell. As it growled again, she blushed from embarrassment.

Tall Moon smiled because he had also heard, but he had brought enough food to fill those empty spaces in her stomach. She could be pleasantly full when she returned to his father's home.

"You look much more comfortable without mud on your face," Tall Moon said in a teasing fashion, smiling as he stepped into the cabin.

His eyes moved slowly over her as he walked nearer. The softness of the doeskin dress defined her every dip and curve, revealing to him that she might be tiny, yet she was perfect in every way.

Her golden hair was clean now and hung in long waves down her back. Her sparkling blue eyes, overshadowed by thick lashes, were gazing back at him, and what he saw in those eyes told him that she was not afraid of him.

He was so glad that she felt comfortable in his presence, as he did in hers.

She was a beautiful, tiny thing, someone he truly wanted to find a way to protect.

But once he returned her to his father's home, her well-being was not under his control.

He didn't like thinking about her being under the same roof as his brother, Darren. Although he had only spoken to his brother for a few moments, it was enough to see what kind of man he was. Darren was an openly callous, snide, uncaring person.

If Tall Moon ever found out that Darren had wronged this woman in any way, Darren would hear from his older brother in a way that would be much different from their first meeting.

Tall Moon would make certain that Darren never bothered Rowena again.

"Yes, I feel much better, thank you," Rowena said softly. She could not help blushing beneath his close scrutiny. "It is a wonderful thing now to be able to smile without thinking my face is going to crack from the mud that had dried on it."

Tall Moon chuckled and went up to her.

He had never felt awkward in the presence of a woman before. But now, just being near Rowena made him feel as though a stranger to himself.

And he knew that was not wise.

Their two worlds could not meet even though he was half white, himself. He had never wanted to be part of that white world again.

But now? He wanted to be with Rowena again. He would do whatever was necessary to make that possible.

She was the woman he desired. He truly wanted to know her better.

"I have brought food," Tall Moon quickly said as he bent to one knee and placed the tray of food on the cattail mats before the fire. "There is soup. There is bread. There is meat. I believe there is enough here for you to choose from."

"It all looks wonderfully delicious," Rowena said, melting inside when he stood up and reached a hand to her elbow. His touch made her breath catch in her throat.

She smiled at him again as he helped her down onto the softness of the mats. Then he sat down himself, on the other side of the tray with its tempting aromas.

When Tall Moon saw her hesitate before choosing what to eat, he picked up one of the two bowls of soup and handed it to her, and then gave her a wooden spoon.

"This soup is one of my peoples' favorites," he said.

She gazed into the bowl, then looked at him questioningly. "It is like no soup that I have ever seen before," she said. "It's . . . it . . . has the consistency of honey, and the bowl isn't warm to the touch. I have never . . . eaten . . . cold soup."

"This soup was made from grapes and cornmeal," Tall Moon gently explained. "It is best eaten while it is cold. Taste it. You shall find it pleasant to your tongue, and it is also very nourishing."

Rowena looked into the bowl again, studying it, for she had never heard of grapes being used in soup before.

Yet it sounded delicious, for she loved grapes.

She scooped up some of the soup with the spoon and was bringing it to her mouth when Tall Moon picked up a piece of bread and placed it on a small platter, then handed this to her, too.

"You will also enjoy *stanica*, the bread made by the Cherokee women," Tall Moon said as she gingerly took the piece he offered her while balancing the bowl of soup on her lap, hoping not to spill it on the lovely, borrowed dress.

"*Stanica*?" she said as she stared at the bread, which was of a soft orange color. She bit off a small bite, her eyes widening in surprise.

"Why, it has the taste of persimmon," she murmured. "Very, very ripe persimmon."

"That is because persimmons are used to make the bread, along with corn that has been pounded fine," Tall Moon said. He was glad that she seemed to be enjoying what he had offered her.

"I do like everything you have given to me," Rowena said, now eagerly eating both the soup and bread.

She watched as Tall Moon got his own bowl of soup and piece of bread and began eagerly eating. They finished both and then Tall Moon offered her meat on another small wooden platter.

"The meat is venison," he said. "In my world, the warriors who choose meat over most other foods are more muscular and strong than those who choose vegetables over meat."

Rowena blushed as she looked at the muscles bulging against his buckskin outfit. She knew that if what he said about eating meat was true, he must have had a healthy diet of venison, for she had never seen a man who was as muscular as Tall Moon.

Nor . . . as handsome.

She could not get enough of gazing at his sculpted features. And his dark eyes seemed to hold mystery and intrigue in them.

Although he was part white, there was not one thing about him that revealed that side of his heritage. In every way, he seemed Indian.

Feeling awkward now in the silence that had fallen suddenly between them, Rowena searched for something to say. She didn't want either of them to feel awkward while they were together.

She did hope that even after she returned to Lawrence's house, she could count on seeing Tall Moon again. She knew that it was not best to anticipate such a meeting, for she was keenly aware of the resentments between Tall Moon and the rest of his family.

Tall Moon might keep his distance from them after he returned her to that world he obviously despised.

"I saw something that mystified me upon my first arrival in your village," Rowena blurted out.

"And what was that?" Tall Moon asked. "Was it something that you saw my people doing?"

"It was a white post that had a white skin of some animal fastened to the top," Rowena said softly. "What is it for? Or is it nothing at all, but

just something children put together while playing games among themselves?"

"No, it was not a thing made up while the children were playing," Tall Moon said, his voice taking on a more serious note. "What you saw is a
reminder for our people. When one or another
gazes at this post, it speaks to them about the danger of forgetting the rules our earliest generation of
Cherokee set down as law. Since then, the Cherokee have followed those rules, which forbid sin-
ning against each other. If these rules are broken
by any of our people, when that person dies, he or
she does not go to the happy place of our people,
but instead will be forever miserable and lost. If a
person lives a clean life, and makes others happy,
he or she goes to a place of pureness . . . of happiness, forevermore."

"Is your people's happy place called heaven?"
Rowena asked. "If so, your people hold a belief in
common with mine. In my world there is heaven
and hell. It is the Bible that teaches right and
wrong to white children, and people of all ages."

"I know about the Bible," Tall Moon said. "Although my father does not seem the sort to pick
up a Bible, there were times when I saw him go
into his study, by himself, and take a Bible from
the long rows of books displayed in his book-
cases. He read verses, but only to himself. He did
not tell me that I must read the Bible, nor did he
instruct my mother to. He knew that my mother's
beliefs were different from his own."

"Tell me, again, please, about your mother, and
how it is that you are here now, and not with your

father and brother," Rowena said, searching his eyes. "But if I am intruding on something personal, I apologize."

"No, there is no need to apologize," Tall Moon said, gazing into the dancing flames of the fire. "My mother was a Cherokee princess, yet her position was not enough to hold her among our people, not after she fell in love with a rich white man. She left her Cherokee home willingly and never returned."

"But you did," Rowena murmured, finding this very interesting.

He gave her a strange look of longing, then gazed into the flames of the fire once again. "I returned to my true roots, to the place where I was meant to be," he said, his voice proud. "After my brother was born, my father sent me away, to live among people whose skin color matched my own. My grandfather, my mother's father, was chief to our Bird Clan of Cherokee at that time. He welcomed me with open arms. I never looked back."

He turned slow eyes to her. "Until recently," he said. "Not until I heard trees being cut so close to my home and followed the sound to the logging camp, where I found my blood kin. It is my father's men who are taking down those trees. I plan to stop them."

"Do you think you can?" Rowena asked, bringing his eyes around to gaze into hers once again. "He has so many men working with him. Do you think he will bring those men to your village and cause your people harm if you insist on his leaving the area?"

"My Cherokee people have been tricked over and over again by the white government," Tall Moon said solemnly. "Many of my Cherokee people died struggling against those white leaders who were taking so much from us. My grandfather died while fighting for his rights. Upon his death, I was named chief. It was under my leadership that what was left of our Bird Clan came to this place where, thus far, no white man has settled."

He shook his head and sighed heavily. "Not until now. And it is my own father and brother who have brought what might be disaster to my people all over again," he said tightly. "I cannot allow that to happen. If blood must be spilled to make my father realize that I will not be pushed around like so many Cherokee before us, then so be it."

He laughed harshly. "Treaties," he said. "You cannot imagine how many so-called treaties were pushed upon my people, only to be broken, as though my people were nothing but trash. I will never be fooled into putting my name on treaty papers. They are all lies."

"I'm so sorry that your people have been mistreated by the white government," Rowena said, truly saddened by how much his people had been made to suffer. "And I'm certain that you will prevail, Tall Moon, for I hear the determination in your voice, and I see it in your eyes."

"I will prevail," Tall Moon said, nodding. "I cannot allow anyone else to bring harm to my people, ever again."

"Yet you brought me here, among them," Rowena said, now realizing just what it must have taken for him to make such a decision. He had to trust her.

"I can see that you are different," Tall Moon said. He dared to reach out and place a gentle hand on the softness of her cheek.

He was not at all surprised when she did not retreat from his touch, but instead, openly accepted it.

"You are someone who has also lost much in your life. I am glad it was not my people who caused the unhappiness I sometimes see in the depths of your eyes," Tall Moon said, his gaze again searching hers.

"No, it was not your people, but that awful war," she said.

She reached up and laid one of her hands on his, relishing this special moment with him. There was so much trust between them, as well as something else.

Love.

Yes, deep inside herself she felt that she was in love with this man, even though she had just met him. She believed that he felt the same about her.

"Our lives were torn apart by the war," she murmured. "The South is all but ruined."

"But being a strong people, you will rebuild your homes," Tall Moon said.

"Just as your people have rebuilt theirs," Rowena said. "I am so sorry about all you have lost."

He took her hand in his as he lowered his other hand from her face. "You have lost so much, yourself, yet you feel such empathy for my people," Tall Moon said thickly. "You are a woman of good heart."

"I try to be," Rowena said, blushing as he held her hand so tenderly. "I . . . try . . . to be."

He wanted so badly to pull her into his arms and kiss her, yet he felt that he had gone as far as he should, since this was their first time alone together.

But he would not let it be their last.

Somehow they would work out how to see each other while he tried to solve this conflict with his father.

"I should return you to my father's home," he said, slowly releasing her hand. "I do not believe it is best to worry him."

"I imagine he already must be wondering where I might have gone, and why I have been away for so long. Yes, I'd better return before it starts to get dark," Rowena said. She softly smiled at Tall Moon as he helped her up from the mats. "I want to thank you again for coming to my rescue. What a mess I was!"

She glanced down at the dress she had on, then looked up at Tall Moon again. "I have no choice but to wear this dress back to Lawrence's house," she murmured. "And to do so will mean that I will have many questions to answer. Will that harm your cause in any way, for him to know that I was with you?"

"Not at all," Tall Moon said. He went to the back of the room and picked up a travel bag.

He walked to where she had discarded her soiled clothes and stuffed them inside the bag, mud dropping to the floor as it flaked from the skirt.

He handed the bag to her. "My father will just have to accept that you have been with me," Tall Moon said firmly.

He took her gently by an elbow. "Now come with me," he said, already walking her toward the door. "I will accompany you to my father's house, but I will not go all the way. I will make certain that you are close enough to be safe. I do not want to come face-to-face with my father again so soon. I have much to put straight in my mind first, and then I must make certain that I also straighten things inside my father's mind. He will be made to understand that what I ask of him must happen."

"I haven't been around him much, but I know that he is a stubborn, determined man," Rowena said, walking outside and stepping up to her horse. "It won't be easy, Tall Moon, to get him to understand your reasoning about the trees. I do think you might have quite a fight on your hands."

"I will not allow my father to be the victor," Tall Moon said. He helped her into her saddle.

He took her bag and attached it to the side of her saddle, then reached up and took one of her hands in his.

"But I now have more than one reason to be careful how I achieve my goal," he said. "For I do not want you to be harmed while I am doing it.

Nor do I want you to do anything that will prevent you and me from knowing each other better."

Again Rowena realized that she was blushing as she gazed down into his eyes. But it was the warm flesh of his hand as he held hers that was making her heart thump wildly in her chest.

Never in her life had a man affected her in this way, not until now, not until Tall Moon!

Their eyes held for a moment longer, and then Tall Moon mounted his own horse.

Together they rode through the village, Rowena feeling eyes on her as Tall Moon's people stopped and stared at her all over again.

She was glad to be away from the village, riding through the forest where it was only herself and Tall Moon. She wished that it could be this way forever and ever.

She cast Tall Moon a soft smile.

"Thank you again," she murmured. "I don't know what I would have done had you not come along to help me."

"*A-a-do*. In my language, that means thank you," he said.

He paused, then added, "I shall always be here if you need help. You know where I live. All you need to do is come, and whatever you want, I shall see that it is yours."

Hearing the confirmation of his feelings for her, Rowena felt safe and loved for the first time since she had said that sad good-bye to her father.

And this was not her father.

This was the man she wanted to be with for the rest of her life.

She only hoped that she wasn't misreading what he had said. She would want to die if she discovered that he was this kind, noble, and sweet to all the women he came across in the forest.

Chapter Fifteen

After putting his horse in the corral, Darren hurried toward his home, hoping that his father hadn't missed him yet. The cursing he heard as he approached the cabin made his eyebrows rise.

It was his father's voice and Darren was afraid that someone had brought word to him about Darren's cockfights. If someone had tattled on Darren, that person wouldn't see the dawn of another day.

He hurried onward.

Just as he stepped out of the shadows of the trees, he saw his father trying to mount his horse, which was something his father hadn't attempted in some time. His father must be terribly upset about something to try it now.

Darren rushed up to his father just as Lawrence slid clumsily again to the ground. His face was beet red, not only from anger, but embarrassment since some of his lumberjacks stood around him, gawking.

Lawrence made a wide turn and glared at the men. "Get outta here!" he shouted. "Do you enjoy watchin' a one-armed man making an ass of himself? Git! Or I'll fire the lot of you."

Darren was truly afraid now of what was making his father so angry besides not being able to mount the horse. If it was the cockfighting, Darren could expect a taste of his father's whip across his back.

His father had used the whip on Darren just once, but Darren had managed to grab the end of the whip, stopping his father. He'd announced that if his father ever did that to him again, he'd kill him. Lawrence had never tried to whip him again.

Lawrence turned then and faced Darren. "Where have you been?" he growled out, his eyes narrowing.

"Why?" was all Darren could say, for he wasn't about to tell him the truth.

If his father already knew, that was one thing. But Darren wasn't going to be the one to let the cat out of the bag about his cockfighting.

"I need you, that's why," Lawrence said. He slapped the horse's reins into Darren's hand. "Rowena hasn't returned home yet. Since you weren't here, I decided to go looking for her myself."

Lawrence turned and glared at the black horse, then turned back to Darren. "As you might imagine, I still can't ride," he said angrily. "I can't even get into the saddle, much less stay in it long enough to go and search for Rowena."

Relieved that his father's anger had nothing to do with cockfighting, Darren stepped over closer to the horse. He ran a hand down its withers, then looked at his father again. "I'll go," he said. "I'll find her."

Lawrence's eyes widened. That Darren had actually volunteered to do something without arguing about it was definitely a positive sign. Of late, Darren seemed to challenge everything that Lawrence asked of him.

"Thanks, son," Lawrence said, stepping away from the horse as Darren mounted it. "I'd hate for something to happen to Rowena after I volunteered to see to her welfare. Thanks for understanding and wanting the same, yourself."

Then another thought came to Lawrence. He stepped up closer to the horse and looked squarely into Darren's eyes. "Son, you'd best not be planning anything besides bringing Rowena home," he said baldly. "Like making a play for her while I'm not there to stop it. Is that why you offered to go search for her?"

"Father, why do you always have to think the worst of me?" Darren asked, having for a moment thought that he had won back some of his father's love.

"Promise me, Darren, that you will find Rowena and bring her home unharmed," Lawrence said, his voice filled with building anger toward this son he would never truly trust again.

For a moment he had forgotten to be wary of his second-born. Of late, Lawrence had not felt completely safe in his son's presence.

It was the way Darren defied him as he looked

Lawrence straight in the eye. It was the sinister smile that Darren often gave him now, as though he had something dark on his mind.

Lawrence hated thinking these things, but until Darren showed him a different side of himself, Lawrence would be careful.

Darren said nothing. "I apologize," Lawrence said when the silence dragged out. "Just make sure Rowena is all right. I'd hate to think I've lost my best friend's daughter only two days into her living with me."

Darren stared at Lawrence, a disgusted look on his face; then he snapped the reins and sank his heels into the flanks of the horse and rode off.

Lawrence watched Darren ride into the shadows of the forest until he couldn't see him any longer. Then, feeling dispirited over so many things, he turned and walked slowly back toward his home.

He took another quick look over his shoulder in the direction Darren had gone, a cold shiver riding his spine. Darren no longer felt like his son.

Downhearted, he went inside his home and suddenly thought of another son. He could not help wondering how it would have been had he not sent his firstborn away?

It seemed that Tall Moon, as he called himself now, was of a much different breed from his second-born.

Of course, he had Indian blood in him, as did Lawrence's second-born, but that was not what Lawrence was thinking of.

By breed, he meant the sort of man his firstborn had become.

He seemed honest, proud, and filled with a wonderful spirit, none of which qualities his younger brother possessed.

"I truly believe I chose the wrong one to send away," he whispered to himself, his head hanging as he slouched down into a thick-cushioned chair.

His gaze fell upon the dancing flames of the fire in the hearth. In those flames the loveliness of his Indian wife's face smiled back at him.

"I did you wrong," he whispered. "I did both you and Tall Moon wrong." He swallowed hard. "Had I to do it over again, things would be different."

Chapter Sixteen

The shadows were lengthening all around her as Rowena rode through the trees with Tall Moon.

She had known she needed to return to Lawrence's home, but she had not realized just how late it was.

When she suddenly heard an approaching horse, she wondered if it was someone from the logging camp come to look for her. A feeling of dread overcame her when she saw that it was Darren.

She only hoped that Lawrence was responsible for his being there, and that he had not come on his own with the same sort of thing on his mind as he had shown her when he placed his hand on her knee beneath the breakfast table.

Tall Moon's jaw clenched when he caught sight of Darren. After last night's unpleasant meeting with his brother, he did not savor a second encounter.

But there he was. Darren drew a tight rein when Rowena and Tall Moon stopped. He glared from one to the other.

"What are you doing with Rowena?" Darren demanded, breaking the silence. His lips twisted into a sneer, and his next words were even more offensive than his glare. "Why haven't you scalped her?"

Darren laughed at his own humor, but his eyes widened when he suddenly noticed that Rowena was wearing the clothes of a savage squaw.

"So my brother has lured you into his clutches, and now you are even wearing the clothes of a squaw?" Darren blurted out.

Tall Moon was holding back, forcing himself not to say things that he knew might incite violence between himself and his brother. He looked quickly over at Rowena as she spoke up on her own behalf.

"Tall Moon came to my rescue after I was thrown from my horse," Rowena said stiffly. She hated having to explain anything to this man whom she despised.

She knew that Darren was trouble, not only for herself, but also for Tall Moon and his people.

Darren smiled sarcastically. "I see no broken bones," he said. "And why would being thrown from a horse require you to wear a squaw's dress?" he asked, his gaze moving slowly over Rowena.

She was intriguingly beautiful in the Indian dress, the soft fabric of the doeskin clinging to her figure. The sight caused an ache in his loins, and he vowed to himself that he would soon have Rowena in his bed.

If his father interfered, it would be the last time Lawrence Ashton tired to order him around.

"Not that it is any of your business, but Tall

Moon found me in the muddy swamp," Rowena said.

She hoped that if she continued talking with Darren, she could diffuse some of the tension between them.

"He found me covered with mud," she explained hastily. "It was even on my face. He took me to his home and offered me water to clean myself, and then gave me this dress and moccasins."

She hoped that what she'd said was enough to stop Darren's sarcastic comments. She hoped that she could return with him to his father's home while Tall Moon went back to his own.

But she knew that if Darren continued his offensive banter, Tall Moon would have enough of it and there would be a confrontation.

She didn't want to be the cause of their coming to blows. All she wanted now was to get back to the cabin and escape to the peacefulness of her room.

If Darren would allow it. She didn't trust him now any farther than she could throw him.

Even the thought of continuing onward through this darkening forest with him made her uncomfortable. Might not Darren take this opportunity, when she and he were alone, to do more than try to touch her knee?

She shivered at the thought of having to fight him off, knowing that she did not have the strength to do so. He was a hefty man.

"My brother rescued you, huh?" Darren said, giving Tall Moon a slow, sly gaze. He then looked into Rowena's eyes again. "Well, it's about time to let a white man assist this lady in distress, don't you think?"

He gestured with a hand toward Rowena. "Come on along with me," he said flatly. "My father is worried about you and he has reason to be since I found you with a damn savage."

Tall Moon had taken enough from his brother. Darren's insults hit him like blows in the gut. He couldn't believe that his own blood kin could talk about him like that.

Yet Tall Moon made himself keep his composure. He did not like the idea of fighting his brother in front of Rowena. He didn't want her to leave remembering that side of him.

Thus far she had seen who he truly was . . . someone who did not try to settle problems by using violence.

He was a man of peace, but with a brother such as Darren, he was finding it very hard to hold back his temper. Darren's disparaging remarks about Indians infuriated him and made him wonder how his brother could forget that he was, in part, Indian, too?

He gazed over at Rowena, whose eyes were flashing with anger as she glared back at Darren. She dismounted and marched up to Darren.

"Darren, must I remind you that you are also a savage if that is what you call someone of Cherokee heritage? Are you not of the same blood as Tall Moon?" she asked, meeting his gaze in a silent battle of wills. "Did you not both have an

Indian woman as a mother? Does not that make you, in part, Indian, yourself? So would you call yourself a savage?"

She leaned closer to him. "Would you?" she taunted. "Are you a savage?"

When he did not respond, but instead only stared blankly at her, Rowena laughed and walked back to her mare, but did not mount Misty again just yet.

She turned and gazed at Darren once more. "I know of only one man here who is a true savage, and, Darren, that is you. Not because you are, in part, Indian, but because you are a horrible man who does not know how to respect blood kin," she said. Her eyes wavered. "If only I had someone from my family left alive that I could love. But I don't. I have had to learn to live without family. Feel blessed, Darren, not cursed, that you have family. You should welcome Tall Moon, not insult him."

"Tall Moon is nothing to me," Darren growled out. "Not now, not ever, and as for having a savage squaw for a mother? I never set eyes on her, so as far as I am concerned, she never existed."

Tall Moon was almost at the breaking point, finding it practically impossible to hold his anger at bay any longer. He longed to slam a fist into Darren's lily white face, yet Tall Moon still kept control of his anger.

"Darren, must I remind you that were it not for our mother, you would not be here today?" Tall Moon said, his voice tight with controlled anger. "Also, must I remind you that our mother died while giving life to you? She sacrificed herself for you, just as Rowena's father sacrificed his life in order that your father and mine would live."

Darren laughed sarcastically. "As far as that rescue goes, it was wasted energy because our father has proved to be utterly worthless," he said, his eyes narrowing as he glared into Tall Moon's.

Even though Tall Moon had no feelings left for his father, he felt it was wrong for his brother to talk so disrespectfully about him. Tall Moon rode his horse quickly up to Darren's.

Before Darren could react, Tall Moon leaped from his horse onto Darren's and grabbed Darren around the throat, pulling him to the ground.

Rowena stepped away from them both, gasping. She covered her mouth with a hand as she watched Tall Moon knock Darren over onto his back, then straddle him.

He held Darren in place by holding his wrists to the ground. "*A-na-da-ni-ti*, I was fortunate that I was raised by a loving mother who taught me right from wrong, and compassion for even those who would wrong me. Otherwise I might kill you for the way you have behaved, and for the ugliness of your words," he growled out.

He leaned down into Darren's face, glad that he saw fear now in his brother's eyes instead of sarcasm.

"You are pushing this older brother to the very edge of what our mother's teachings meant," he went on, glaring into his brother's eyes that were the same color as their father's, instead of the dark brown of their mother's. "Our mother would be very embarrassed to know you as a son, just as I am embarrassed to know you as my *a-na-da-ni-ti*."

He tightened his hands on Darren's wrists. "Listen well to what I say to you today," Tall Moon commanded, his eyes gleaming into Darren's. "If you cause Rowena distress of any kind, I will make you pay."

He ran his fingers through his brother's fiery red hair, which he had inherited from their father's side of the family. "Brother, your red hair would make a very colorful addition to my scalp pole," he taunted, thinking to himself that of course he had no scalp pole in his home, nor did any of his people have such a thing of dishonor in theirs.

At just the thought of being scalped, Darren turned his head aside and vomited.

Rowena gasped and recoiled at the sight. She had never seen a man so afraid and humiliated at the same time.

She stopped herself from smiling at Tall Moon's reference to a scalp pole in his home. Well, she had been there and she had seen no scalp pole.

Tall Moon stood up, leaving Darren to wipe the remains of the vomit from the sides of his mouth with the sleeve of his shirt.

Tall Moon went to Rowena and placed gentle hands on her waist. "Are you going to be all right?" he asked, searching her eyes.

"I'll be just fine," she murmured, reveling in his touch. "*A-a-do*, thank you again for all that you have done for me."

Tall Moon's eyes widened at Rowena's use of the Cherokee word for "thank you," pleased that she had remembered the word.

Her knees almost buckled when he brought one of his hands to her cheek and laid it gently there as their eyes met and held.

Then he turned and mounted Magic, gave Darren a look of warning, and rode off into the falling darkness of the forest.

Rowena turned and stood over Darren. He seemed a broken man, but she was afraid that would last for only a moment. Oh, surely he would find a way to make Tall Moon pay for this humiliation.

Not waiting for Darren to get up and go to his horse, Rowena quickly mounted Misty and rode off in the direction of the cabin. She knew that it wasn't far away now, for she could smell the aroma of food cooking over the stove in the kitchen.

She sank her heels into Misty's flanks and hurried onward, sighing with relief when she finally saw the house, lamplight glowing from its windows.

Although this was not truly her home, and never would be, at least for now she had a safe haven.

She rode up to the corral and guided her horse inside, dismounted, then hurried into the cabin and to her room, without even telling Lawrence that she was back. She knew Darren would tell his father that he had found her.

She wanted quiet now, not talk.

She went to the bedroom window as she heard an approaching horse outside. She laughed to herself when Darren did come into view. He looked a beaten man, hunched over in the saddle and disheveled from his fight with Tall Moon.

"Perhaps he's learned a lesson?" she whispered to herself, recalling the fear in Darren's eyes when Tall Moon was straddling him.

She shivered at the thought of how Darren seemed to hate not only Tall Moon, but also her. She even believed that he hated his own father.

Chapter Seventeen

It had been hard to get through the evening meal with all of the men gawking at Rowena again. Though she was seated between Darren and Lawrence, she did not feel at all safe.

At least Lawrence hadn't made an issue over her being gone for so long today. She hadn't wanted to tell him about being with Tall Moon.

And she didn't expect Darren to tell him, either, because it had been evident to her that Tall Moon had put the fear of God in this man's heart. No, she didn't think that Lawrence would ever find out where she had been today.

She was glad of that fact because she planned to go to the Indian village again. She ached to see Tall Moon, and soon.

Again her thoughts returned to Lawrence. When he had come to her bedroom door after she had changed into one of her own dresses, he had only told her that he was glad she was all right. Then he had asked her to please join him and Darren at the supper table.

That was the last thing she wanted to do, since

she would be eating with those horrible lumber-jacks, but she knew that she had to get used to it as long as she was living at Lawrence's house.

Once the meal was over Darren hurried out of the cabin and Rowena went into the study with Lawrence upon his invitation.

Because she had caused him such concern today by staying out much longer than she had meant to, she felt that she somehow needed to make things up to him.

She had begun to worry about him, for the more she was around him, the more she realized that he was not a well man.

Of course he had the strength to shout out his orders to the men who worked for him, but he seemed too weak to do much else. She knew that weakness was because of the war. It had taken not only his arm from him, but a lot of the energy that he had had during his younger years.

Wanting to help lift his spirits, and recalling his interest in her violin, Rowena had brought it to the study.

Lawrence sat slouched in the deep cushions of a chair only a few feet from the leather sofa, on which Rowena was sitting. Both of them faced a roaring fire in the hearth.

Lawrence had just lit his pipe and was puffing easily on it, occasionally clacking his teeth against its wooden stem. Seeing him enjoying his pipe so much, Rowena recalled with an aching heart her father doing the same.

He had loved to smoke before a grand fire in their parlor in the evenings. Her mother would be embroidering some pretty pillowcase while Rowena read one of her favorite novels about romance.

In her mind's eye, she had envisioned the handsome prince that she was reading about coming to life and falling in love with her. She had hoped to meet such a prince one day, and now she felt she had, in Tall Moon.

In a sense, as leader of his people, he was a prince. Certainly, he was as handsome as any storybook hero.

"I'm glad you brought your violin to the study," Lawrence said, crossing his legs at his ankles as he stretched them out before him. "Will you play me a piece, Rowena? That would be a perfect way to end my day."

"I would love to," Rowena murmured.

She stood and went to where she had left her violin case resting on a table.

She unsnapped it and raised the lid, the smell of rosin and the varnished wood of her violin wafting to her nose. Again memories of her past rose up.

Oh, how her parents had loved to hear her play, even when she had just begun to learn. As each year passed, her skill grew until finally she had fulfilled the promise of her talent.

She had pressed into a scrapbook several blue ribbons that she had won while playing her violin in regional contests. Sadly, the book had been lost, as well as everything else she loved, when the Yankees' fire swept her home, destroying everything in its path.

She was so glad that her father had placed her violin case among the meager belongings that she had taken to the convent with her. Had she lost her violin in that fire, it would have been like losing a part of her heart.

She loved the feel of her violin against her hand as she lifted it from the case. She plucked each string, to test whether all were in tune.

When she found her E string slightly off-key, she tightened it, then plucked it with her finger again, smiling when she heard a perfect tone this time.

She laid the violin down on the table, then took the bow from the case and tightened it.

As she had done so many times before in her life, she picked up the square of rosin and ran her bow across it, back and forth, until she felt there was enough new rosin on her bow to make it move like magic across the strings as she played.

She laid the rosin back inside her case, then tucked the chin rest of the violin beneath her chin. Placing the bow on her strings, she stretched her tiny fingers into position and began to play.

Lovely music poured from the violin as she drew the bow back and forth across the strings, her fingers finding the right places on the strings to make exactly the sound she wished for. She began playing "Courante," a song she had performed as a duet with a friend at a contest before the war.

She and her friend Nadine had won first place that day, and were each awarded a blue ribbon as well as a medal. Her medal was tucked away in her violin case. She only wished now that she had placed the ribbon with it.

As she played she glanced over at Lawrence. His eyes were closed, yet his pipe was still clamped between his teeth, the smoke slowly spiraling from its bowl. The aroma was the same as her father's tobacco.

Tears came to her eyes as she pictured her father resting before the fire, listening to her playing. She closed her own eyes for a second or two, imagining that the tobacco she was smelling now was coming from her father's pipe and that it was he, not Lawrence, who sat before the fire, listening.

But reality returned when she heard the loud laughter of men outside the study window. She again remembered where she was, and for whom she played the violin. She was so glad that Lawrence hadn't pressed her for answers about where she'd gone today.

She wondered why he hadn't asked?

Surely it was because he did not want to make her uncomfortable by prying into her life. He had done his duty to his friend by giving her a home. But apparently he didn't want to make her feel as though she would always be accountable to him now that she shared his roof.

Again her thoughts returned to her best friend, Nadine.

Since they had not seen each other since she'd left for the convent, she had often wondered what had become of her best friend. She hoped that Nadine and her family had made it through the horrors of the war.

Rowena stopped playing and turned quickly when she heard someone enter the room. She found Darren standing there, leaning against the door frame, a cigar resting in the corner of his mouth.

"Don't stop on my account," Darren said mockingly as she took her bow from the violin strings. "But know that I think it's just a lot of racket you are making on that thing. But if my father wants to listen, so be it."

"Thank you for your permission," Rowena said sarcastically.

She turned away from him. Even though her heart was no longer in playing her violin, since a man she despised was now listening to her, for Lawrence's sake she did continue to play.

Lawrence had listened so intently, she knew that the music had brought him a few moments of relaxation and enjoyment.

Darren continued leering at Rowena as she began to play again. He hated her now with a passion because she had witnessed his moments of humiliation at the hands of his savage brother.

Oh, how he abhorred Tall Moon.

Oh, how he hoped to find a way to make him pay for what he had done today. The humiliation still made his insides twist with fury.

Yes, somehow, he would avenge what had been done to him, and it had just come to him that he would find his revenge against his brother through this woman. It had been very evident that his brother was in love with her!

Darren would be certain that his brother never had her.

But tonight he had other things on his mind. Enough time had passed for the men to get settled in the clearing as they waited to see another cockfight. Anticipating this victory, Darren hurriedly left the room and rushed outside.

His gait hastened the closer he got to the clearing. He was eager to watch his prized cocks kill their opponents in the ring. Good ol' Lloyd would be the one to have to toss his feathered friends into the bushes, dead as doornails.

He threw his head back in raucous laughter, amused by the thought of what his cocks would do to Lloyd's.

Now that he was far enough from the cabin that his father would not be able to hear him, Darren began shouting Lloyd's name until his friend came and met him halfway.

"Ready to lose a cock tonight?" Darren asked, his eyes dancing with mischief.

"No, but I hope you are," Lloyd said, clasping a hefty arm around Darren's shoulder as they walked onward. "Come on. We've waited long enough. The men have their money out in their hands, ready to make their bets."

"That's what it's all about," Darren said, laughing loudly. "The big green. I'm gonna win me a fistful of the big green tonight."

Lloyd gave him a frown, then stepped away from Darren and ran on ahead, to where the cocks were pacing in their cages.

Darren stepped up to the ring of men, then pushed his way through them.

He stopped and stared at his prized cock, which strutted in its cage, its eyes dark, its neck stretched long as it gazed into the cage sitting opposite his.

In it was another cock.

Lloyd's.

Darren smiled wickedly as he thought of where Lloyd's cock would be soon. Dead and thrown aside like a soiled, limp dishrag!

Chapter Eighteen

Dressed in riding attire, a skirt and blouse, and her last pair of boots, since her others had been ruined by mud, Rowena rode Misty beneath the white sheen of the moon.

It was as though she was answering the call of the wild, following it into the forest. An owl called into the night with its strange hoot-hooting. She heard the faraway howling of coyotes.

But she didn't fear either the coyotes or the owl. Her true fear and the cause of her uneasiness was back at the cabin. She hoped Darren was fast asleep and unaware of her being out alone in the night.

She rode onward into the forest where the moon's glow was hidden except when it filtered through the foliage of the trees overhead. She welcomed its meager light in the forbiddingly dark forest.

Yet she didn't want to turn back toward the place she had been told to call home. Lawrence Ashton's cabin was nothing like the only true home she had known . . . the one she had shared with her mother and father.

She felt so dispirited in the logging camp, so alone. Out here on her horse she felt more comfortable.

She loved riding Misty. She could pretend she was back in Georgia, taking a moonlight ride before going home, to climb into her thick, wonderfully soft, feather bed, knowing that her mother and father lay in a room only footsteps away down the corridor.

She had always felt so safe with her father nearby.

But her home, her family, her sense of security had all been robbed from her. . . .

Suddenly her thoughts were interrupted when she heard something quite strange coming from the depths of the forest.

She stopped, her heart racing with fear. She heard the sounds of men laughing and cheering, as though they were watching some sort of game.

She only now realized just how far she had gone from the camp. She had traveled much farther into the forest than she had planned.

Always curious, Rowena ignored the voice that told her to turn her horse back in the direction of Lawrence's cabin.

The laughter continued, and the men's voices now came to her more clearly. She heard someone say, "Come on, fight, damn it."

"I've got to see," she whispered to herself, sliding quickly from her saddle. She tied her reins to a tree, then tiptoed onward toward the sound of the men's voices. She stopped dead in her tracks when she saw lamplight glowing through a break in the trees just up ahead.

The voices were loud, even boisterous. And then she recognized one of them.

Her knees weakened when she realized it was Darren's voice. She had been wrong to assume that he would retire to his room so early in the evening, when the moon had not so long ago replaced the sun in the sky.

Hearing his voice and knowing she must be especially careful not to be caught, Rowena cautiously moved onward until she finally came close enough to see what was happening.

From the edge of the trees she could see the men gathered in a clearing, and though it was difficult to make out what they were watching, she could hear the squawking of chickens. Goose bumps traveled across Rowena's flesh, for she now knew that what was transpiring here tonight was undoubtedly a cockfight.

She had heard about cockfights back in Georgia, but had never seen any, nor had she ever wanted to, because she knew of the viciousness that was associated with the sport.

Her father had told her one evening, while sitting comfortably before a lazy fire, about something that he had heard was happening not many miles from their plantation. He had told her that someone had brought cockfighting into the area, and since she had never heard of such a thing, he had explained to her all that he knew.

She had been told enough to know the evils of

these horrible fights. Again a small voice inside Rowena's brain told her to turn around and leave.

But she needed to see exactly who was involved in this, for she most certainly was going to report this to Lawrence tomorrow.

She peered at the men's faces, but it was difficult to recognize any of them in the moonlight. Then the crowd shifted and she caught sight of the roosters fighting. They were both covered with blood and looked half dead. Rowena turned her eyes away.

She fought back the urge to vomit, knowing that the sound would alert the men to her presence. While she struggled to control her reaction, Darren stepped into full view, fortunately with his back to her. His fists were in the air as he goaded the roosters on, cursing them with vile words Rowena had never heard before.

She watched him for a moment longer, then turned and ran blindly into the dark, forgetting that she had arrived on Misty.

All that she could think about now was getting as far away from this hideous scene as possible, for if she inhaled deeply enough, she could actually smell the blood that was being spilled behind her in the fighting arena. And Darren had seemed almost demonic as he shouted and swung his fists in the air.

Sobbing now, not understanding how anyone could be so cruel as to encourage two animals to kill each other, Rowena kept on running, then suddenly collided with someone.

Stifling a scream of fear behind her hand, she

turned and ran in another direction. Had one of the men seen and followed her?

When she heard footsteps gaining on her from behind, and then felt a hand grab her by the wrist, Rowena almost fainted. Her eyes were wide with terror as she was swung around to face her captor.

There was enough moonlight sifting through the foliage overhead for her to see the face of her assailant. She was flooded with relief when she saw who it was.

Tall Moon!

He drew her into a quick embrace and comforted her when he felt her trembling.

"What are you doing out here, alone?" he asked, still holding her as she trembled against his hard body.

Rowena felt wonderfully safe in his arms, but she could not forget the sight of those two roosters fighting each other, blood all over feathers that had surely been beautiful before the fight began.

"You saw it, too, didn't you?" Tall Moon said, gently stroking her back through her cotton blouse. "I was out riding tonight when I heard a commotion. I went close enough to see what was happening. I discovered the cockfighting."

"I . . . did, too," Rowena sobbed out. "It was so horrible. And . . . and . . . Darren is involved. I think he might even be the instigator of it. He has to be. The ones with him are the lumberjacks who work for him and his father."

She eased out of his arms, although she hated to leave his tender embrace. But she wanted to see him, not only feel him.

She gazed into his midnight-dark eyes, made even more hauntingly beautiful by the moonlight sifting through the leaves overhead.

"It is so heartless," she said, swallowing hard. "I knew there was such a thing as cockfighting because it went on in Georgia, on the outskirts of Atlanta. My father explained it to me, the heartlessness of it."

"I, too, had heard about such a thing, but had never seen it actually happening, not until tonight," Tall Moon said, holding one of her hands. "That my blood kin is a part of such evil makes me again wonder how it is that two brothers can be so different."

"You are who you are because of your mother's teachings," Rowena murmured, recalling what he'd said about the relationship between him and his Indian mother. "Your brother was not as fortunate as you. He has been raised with bitterness and evil in his heart. I . . . I . . . believe he can never be anything different."

She eased back into his arms and savored his closeness, his kindness. "I am so glad that you are who you are," she said softly. "I feel so blessed to have been found by you after my fall from my horse. Had it been Darren . . ."

"Do not think of him anymore tonight. Try to put your memories of what we both saw somewhere far in the recesses of your mind," Tall Moon softly encouraged.

He was so happy that she had moved back into his arms on her own initiative. She did trust him, and perhaps felt even more than that.

The spirits had led him to her earlier for a reason, and now he knew why.

He had been without a woman for too long, and even though this woman's skin was white, he felt they were meant to be together. They both needed the same thing.

They needed each other!

"I shall try to forget what I saw, but I'm not sure I really can," Rowena murmured. "I may never forget the pained cries of those birds, or the sight of the blood."

"In time, you will forget, because your life was not meant to be filled with such ugliness," Tall Moon said softly. "You were born to enjoy the goodness of life, not the bad."

"There is no good in what is happening back there," she said, trying hard to block the memory from her mind.

She had to admit it seemed to be getting easier. The longer he held her, the more her thoughts were consumed by the wonder of knowing him.

Although they had just met, she knew that she was already in love with this wonderful man.

She had heard of love at first sight.

She had scoffed at the notion before.

But now? She knew it was possible.

It didn't matter to her at all that he was part Cherokee. Tall Moon was gentler and more considerate and loving than most white men she had known.

"Come," Tall Moon said, hating to have to end these gentle moments between them. He longed to explore the depths of their relationship. "I want to take you away from this place of evil. The moonlight is meant to capture your beauty, not the ugliness of what is happening in that fighting arena."

At those words, Rowena's heart soared. The more they were together, the more she believed that his feelings matched hers for him.

While she was with him like this, she did not want to think about what Darren was involved in. For the moment, there was only Tall Moon.

Tall Moon held his arm around her waist and whisked her farther away from the noise of the cheering men and the squawking of the birds.

He walked her to where he had tethered his horse. "You could not have come this far from the cabin on foot," he observed. "Where did you leave your horse? I will take you there."

"It's not far," Rowena said, sighing as he placed his hands at her waist and lifted her onto his saddle. "I shall show you."

He mounted behind her, then with a finger on her chin, turned her face toward him. "Are you going to be all right?" he asked, his eyes searching hers.

"I'm bit shaky, but I'll be all right," she said, smiling at him. "I guess you have rescued me a second time."

"Do you not know by now that I will always be your rescuer?" he asked. "All you need to do is think of me and I will hear your beckoning call and come to you."

Their eyes locked for a moment. Then with a pounding heart, Rowena turned away from him just as he snapped his reins and urged his horse through the trees.

When they reached Misty, Rowena slid from Tall Moon's saddle and went to unwrap Misty's reins from around the limb. Then she mounted the mare and edged over closer to Tall Moon.

"I will escort you to my father's home," he said, reaching out and placing a hand on her cheek. He realized that she leaned her cheek into the warmth of his palm before he moved his hand away.

"We'd best go," she murmured. "If Darren senses we are near, who knows what he might do?"

"He is too immersed in the fighting to think about anything or anybody else," Tall Moon said, riding alongside her on his steed as she made her way slowly through the forest.

Before long Rowena spotted the lamp in her bedroom window, which she had left lit for her return.

She halted her mount as Tall Moon did the same beside her. "*A-a-do*, thank you, Tall Moon, for rescuing me again," she murmured. "I have to ask. What are you going to do about what you saw tonight?"

"I have much to think about," Tall Moon said tightly. He dismounted and helped her from her saddle, then wrapped his arms around her and held her close, leaving only enough space between them so they could look into each other's eyes. "My father and brother have brought nothing but trouble to this area. First cutting the noble trees of the forest and now tormenting these poor birds.

You must be wary of my brother now, even more than before. I feel that you are in danger. Be careful. My brother is a man who reeks of evil."

"My first thought was to go to Lawrence," Rowena said, searching his eyes. "But should Darren discover what I am doing before—"

He placed a gentle hand over her lips, stopping her from speaking further. "Do not put yourself in danger," he said thickly. "I will find a way to stop this madness. You try to act as though nothing has happened when you are with Darren. Can you do that?"

"If I must, yes, I am sure I can," Rowena said, nodding. "But it will be hard. I loathe the man and everything he stands for."

"My feelings are the same," Tall Moon said. "For now, remember . . . silence. Only silence."

She smiled softly and nodded.

He lowered his lips to hers and gave her a kiss that was passionate, yet sweet. Rowena's knees almost buckled from the feeling of desire that swept through her.

In the next moment, he moved away from her, mounted his horse, and was quickly lost to sight in the darkness of the forest.

She reached her fingers up and touched lips that were still warm from his kiss.

She was filled with conflicting feelings. Tonight she had seen the ugly side of life, and also experienced the good.

She made herself continue to think about the good as she put her horse in the corral, then went and sat on the porch to calm herself before going up to bed.

So much had happened tonight . . . some things horrendously bad, and some so very, very wonderful.

Chapter Nineteen

Darren stood just inside the darkness of the forest as he watched Rowena sit down on the steps of the front porch. Ever since he'd spotted her near the cockfighting arena, slow anger had been building inside him.

At the time, he had not wanted to stop and warn her to keep quiet about what she had seen. His cock had been close to tearing the hell out of Lloyd's, and Darren always wanted to be there at the moment of final conquest.

But he had left as soon as he could, and with a plan that he knew would scare her out of reporting to his father what she had seen.

Now he had to make it inside the house without her seeing him, for he had to act in secret. When she saw to what extent he would go, she would realize that she must keep quiet about his activities, or else.

Yes, he knew he must put the fear of God in her in order to keep her from telling his father what she had seen.

He glanced up at his father's bedroom window

and saw no lamplight. He looked at the study windows and saw no lamplight there, either.

He smiled to himself, for he knew that his father was fast asleep by now and would not have any idea of what was transpiring between Darren and the beautiful young woman his father had taken under his wing so foolishly. His father most certainly didn't need a woman around all of these men to stir up trouble among them.

After tonight, Darren couldn't allow her to remain in the logging camp any longer. After tonight, she would want to leave. And then soon, very soon, Darren would have everything exactly as he wanted it. For he had another plan to put in motion, one that involved his father.

Seeing that Rowena was lost in thought as she sat there on the porch, Darren waited for the clouds to slide over the moon so that he would have the cover of darkness to sneak inside. While he waited, Darren thought back to the cockfight.

He smiled crookedly as he saw in his mind's eye how powerful his cock had been. It had quickly established its dominance in the arena, its eyes wild, its razor-sharp spurs inflicting damage the moment the two cocks had been put together.

He would never forget the look on Lloyd's face when he saw that his favorite cock was being defeated.

Only when the final blow was struck, downing Lloyd's prized cock, did Darren consider leaving to do what must be done.

He had a woman to take care of.

The clouds were slowly sliding over the moon now, giving Darren the chance to bolt free of the trees at the back side of the cabin. When he reached the back door, he stopped to get his breath.

Breathing hard, the look of the devil in his green eyes, he leaned against the door.

Then with an evil grin, he hurried inside the house, avoiding the light from the lamp in the parlor as he rushed down the corridor. When he reached the staircase, he took the steps two at a time until he was on the second-floor landing.

There he stopped and listened for any sound in the house. Amos usually did some last chores before retiring for the night.

He glanced toward the door that led into Amos's bedroom. He saw a streamer of light coming from beneath it and knew for certain that Amos was inside.

Darren would have the run of the house now until Rowena decided to come up to bed, which she might at any moment now. Realizing he didn't have much time, Darren went to Rowena's closed bedroom door.

He saw faint light at the bottom of the door, but knew it wasn't because she was inside. He had left her sitting on the porch, probably contemplating what she should do about what she'd seen.

Did she plan to awaken his father with the news? Or would she wait until morning?

If Darren had his way, it would be neither. His plan had to work!

He placed his hand on the doorknob of Rowena's bedroom door, then slowly opened it.

He winced when it gave a faint squeak, but luckily it was not loud enough to bring Amos from his room.

Once he was inside Rowena's bedroom, Darren slowly, carefully, closed the door, then looked quickly around the room.

He smiled when he spied the violin case that sat on a bench at the foot of the bed. It was closed. He hoped that it wasn't locked, for he would have no idea where to look for the key.

He hurried to it and smiled triumphantly when he found the case unlocked. He lifted the lid and gazed down at the violin. It lay in a bed of green velvet.

The smell of the square of rosin lying beside the violin wafted up, causing his nose to twitch.

The smell of varnish was strong, too, and the violin shone with it.

His smile became wicked as he gazed at the violin's strings. They were perfectly in tune after her playing this evening.

He remembered her standing there with the violin tucked beneath her chin, her fingers on the strings, ready to play.

He had to admit to himself that she had played a pretty tune on that violin, but after tonight, she'd never be able to do so ever again. When he got done with her violin, there would be no fixin' it.

His eyes danced at the thought of what he was going to do and what Rowena's reaction would be. She would scream out with anger, and then surely cry, when she saw what he'd done to her precious violin.

With a grunt of anger, he reached down and ripped the strings from the violin. Snickering, he shoved the strings into the front pockets of his breeches.

Then he picked the violin up from its resting place and put it on the floor. His eyes gleaming, he stomped on the violin, over and over again. Wood splinters flew in all directions.

He knew that when Rowena figured out who was responsible for destroying her violin, she would be scared out of her wits. She would realize that he was not a man to cross.

He stepped back and gazed down at the pieces of the violin. He decided he had one more thing to do.

He reached inside the case and picked up the cake of rosin, dropped it on the floor, then ground the heel of his shoe into it until it was mashed flat into the carpet.

Having finished his destruction, he hurried from the room, and scampered down the stairs. Before going outside to join Rowena on the porch, he shoved his hand into his pocket and closed his fingers around the strings with a smile.

Rowena had been making over the events of the night, struggling to decide what she should do. There was something so evil about Darren, she was longing to tell his father what he was doing behind his back.

Yet the longer she sat there, thinking about it, the more she felt she ought to wait and let Tall Moon take charge of the situation. She hoped that he would act soon. What was happening to those poor roosters was so awful, it made bitter bile rise into her throat, almost choking her.

She cleared her throat and then jumped with alarm and stood up quickly when Darren stepped into view on the step beside her.

She slowly rose to her feet. As she backed away from him he snickered and smiled what surely was the most evil, twisted smile she had ever seen. She knew that the color had drained from her face.

"What do you want?" she asked, her voice weak with building fear.

When he didn't respond to her question, she backed as far as she could from him without actually falling off the step. She reached deep inside herself to find the courage to shoot him a look of defiance, but she was so afraid, her knees felt as though they might buckle beneath her.

"What do I want?" Darren mocked, taking a step toward her. "Now, that might depend on you, little woman."

"What . . . do . . . you mean?" Rowena asked, her voice breaking.

"I think you know," Darren said darkly.

"No, I truly don't," Rowena said.

"Well, then, let me refresh your mind just a mite," Darren retorted. "I know you were there tonight. I know that you found the cockfight arena and you must have guessed that it is mine."

He leaned his face into hers, making her tremble at his nearness.

"You're a busybody," Darren said tightly. "Do you know what happens to busybodies?"

Rowena's heart was pounding so hard, she felt as though she might faint. But she found something deep within herself that gave her the courage to stand up to him.

"Darren, how could you have anything to do with such a horrible thing as . . . as . . . cockfighting?" Rowena blurted out. "Darren, were your father to know—"

He interrupted her, moving even closer to her. "And how is he to find out?" he demanded. "You're not going to tell him, are you? You must realize I won't tolerate that. Rowena, you do know that I won't allow you to do something as dumb as that?"

"How . . . are . . . you going to stop me?" Rowena asked, feeling braver by the minute.

"How?" Darren repeated, laughing throatily. "Now, do you really want to know? Or are you playing games with me?"

"Darren, I can't allow you to continue to do something your father would definitely not approve of," Rowena said, placing her fists on her hips.

"You sure are brave tonight, Rowena," Darren said, again laughing mockingly. "Now, what can I do about that? What can I do to shut you up?"

"Nothing," Rowena said, taking a quick step up, toward the porch. "Absolutely nothing."

She turned and faced him again. He was still standing on the lower step, so they confronted each other almost eye-to-eye.

"You don't frighten me, Darren," she spat.

"You have no idea what I can do when I want something," Darren said, sliding a hand inside his breeches pocket. "I have already done something to prove this to you. Go to your room. You will find out what I have done as soon as you enter. That should be warning enough to convince you not to tattle to my father. I wouldn't want to think what I might have to do next time."

"What have you done?" Rowena asked, searching his eyes anxiously.

"Just know that your life lies in your own hands, Rowena," Darren said smugly. "Go to your room. You will see just what I mean."

Suddenly he yanked something from his pocket and held it directly in her face.

"Isn't this proof enough that I mean business?" he gloated. "This should tell you that if you go to my father about what you saw, or about what I have done to you tonight, I'll do worse than break a mere violin to prove my point."

Rowena was stunned by what he held in his hand: the strings to her violin. Suddenly finding it hard to breathe, she placed her hands at her throat.

"Oh, Lord, what have you done?" she finally found the breath to say.

Tears fell from her eyes and rolled in streams down her cheeks.

She hated to think how he had left her violin.

Oh, surely he wouldn't . . .

Darren grabbed her by a wrist. "Compose yourself," he said dryly. "I can't allow you to wake my father up. At least not yet. I want you to see, firsthand, what I've done to your violin. I want you to understand that my warnings are real."

She yanked her arm free and wiped the tears

from her cheeks with her palms. Then suddenly she kicked Darren hard in the leg.

She ran away from him, stumbled into the house, and could hardly get up the stairs quickly enough so that she could see what he had done. She prayed to herself that he had only removed the strings from her violin. Putting them back on would be easy.

But if he had done worse, oh, Lord, she wasn't sure she could continue to live under the same roof with a man such as he.

When she finally got to her room and saw the remains of her violin strewn across the floor, she crumpled to the carpet. He had smashed the violin into a million splinters of wood. She gathered some of the larger pieces together and held them in her arms and cried.

She now knew for certain that Darren was a madman.

She was deathly afraid of him, and she was afraid for Lawrence. Surely he was in danger . . . and from his own son.

Yet now that she knew what Darren was capable of doing, she realized she couldn't go to Lawrence. She was even afraid that somehow Darren would find out if she told Tall Moon.

She felt as though she were caught in a trap and just couldn't fight her way free!

She gazed from the window and into the dark heavens. "Mama, Papa, oh, what am I to do?" she whispered as tears filled her eyes once again. "I . . . am . . . so afraid!"

She had known fear in her life during the war,

but tonight she was terrified. Her terror seemed to cut through to the very core of her being.

Then she saw something else on the carpet. It was something golden mashed into the fabric.

"My rosin," she gulped out. "He left nothing of my violin except the case."

Hatred such as she had never known before, not even for the damn Yankees, swept through her. She had to find the courage to face another day, and then another, and another.

"And I shall!" she whispered, already feeling the strength of the courage she had always known renew itself inside her heart.

"I shall!"

Chapter Twenty

Still reeling from the repulsive sight of the cock-fight, and regretting that his own brother was responsible, Tall Moon rode into his village.

After placing his horse in the corral, he strode immediately to the village chicken pen and went inside. He went to the corner where golden chicks were snuggled together, sleeping peacefully. Careful not to awaken them, Tall Moon ran his fingers across one of the chick's soft, yellow feathers.

Such innocence was there at his fingertips.

Those roosters he had seen tonight had once been as tiny, as innocent, and as sweet.

But because of the evil and greed of his brother, and the other men who were there with him tonight, those beautiful chicks had been turned into violent roosters that were trained to kill. What a horrible existence they had, fighting for their lives as men watched, cheering them on, money in both their hands and pockets, betting on those poor victims.

As the moon's glow fell upon the golden feathers of the tiny chicks, Tall Moon was reminded of

Rowena's soft, golden hair, and how it had felt to hold her in his arms. How wonderful it had been to kiss her, and feel her return the kiss with the same passion as he had felt.

He hated to think of Rowena living under the same roof as his brother. Darren was heartless, crude, cold, and conniving.

Still deep in thought, Tall Moon stepped away from the chicken pen and walked slowly toward his home. He was still uncertain just how he felt about his father. Yes, his *ah-te* had ignored Tall Moon's plea to move his lumber business elsewhere. But Tall Moon sensed that his *father* needed the love of a son. It was evident that Darren had no feelings for him, except loathing, resentment, and hate.

Tall Moon stopped and looked around himself, at the peacefulness of his village.

A few elderly men were sitting by an outside fire, smoking their long-stemmed pipes and talking softly among each other, surely about the past, since there was hardly any future left for them. Their flesh was stretched tightly across their brittle bones, their dark eyes sunk deeply into their faces.

Ah, *ho*, yes, those men had much to discuss, the love of those whom they had lost in one way or another, and what lay ahead when their last breaths on this earth were taken.

Tall Moon knew that some of those elderly men prayed to die soon, before they became a burden to their families, and also because they could hardly wait to join the loved ones who had gone on before them.

The Cherokee believed in an afterlife of happiness and renewal, in which they would be reunited with those who had left this world prematurely.

When he heard a low laugh come from one of those old men, he had to smile, himself, glad that they still took pleasure in this life.

The eerie cry of a loon down by the river made Tall Moon look in that direction. He smiled when he heard another loon responding to the one that had just called.

He went inside his cabin, where a fire burned low, the fallen embers beneath the grate casting an orange glow over the walls and ceiling of his home. Still lost in thought, he put a fresh log on the fire and sat on the mats in front of the hearth. Soon the fire burned high, sending sparks and smoke up the stone chimney.

Tall Moon could not put from his mind what he had seen his brother doing tonight. Darren's pleasure in the violence and blood of the cockfight seemed almost diabolical. *Ho*, it did seem that his brother was *u-yo-I*, no good, and capable of real evil.

It was sad that Darren had not had the opportunity to have been taught goodness by his mother, as Tall Moon had. It was because of his mother that Tall Moon knew how to fill his days with kindness and caring. His brother had no use for either.

Ho, it was a mother's teachings that had been

lacking in his brother's life. And obviously, Darren had not paid heed to anything his father had tried to teach him, for Tall Moon knew that his father was not an evil man.

His *ah-te* had made mistakes in his life—turning away from his wife, disowning his son—but he was not truly evil. This lumber business was another mistake.

His father had always enjoyed being wealthy . . . a rich man. The Civil War had stolen much of that wealth from him, and it seemed that he was trying as hard as he could to get that wealth back.

Tall Moon did not understand that craving for wealth. After a man was put in the ground, he could not carry wealth into the heavens with him.

Suddenly Tall Moon's spine stiffened. He had a sudden, strange feeling, and in his mind's eye he experienced a vision. He saw his father's soft, green eyes, and in them was a look of keen fear!

A cold chill rode his spine when he recalled another vision that he had experienced a few days ago. In this vision a fox, after running a few steps away from Tall Moon, stopped suddenly, looked back at him, and barked.

When a vision such as that came to a Cherokee, it was a sign, a warning to the one who had witnessed it. It meant that one of this person's family members would die soon after.

Would . . . it . . . be Tall Moon's *ah-te* who would die?

Tall Moon had had visions before and what he had seen had proved true.

This fear Tall Moon had seen in his father's eyes, could it have to do with Darren? Or did Lawrence fear his Cherokee son?

Could his father actually believe that Tall Moon would harm him in order to drive him out of the area? Did his father see all Indians as heathens and murderers?

Tall Moon was not sure what to do about these sudden feelings and visions.

Pray.

Ho, that was all that he could do at this moment . . . pray for the Great Spirit to guide him to do right by his father and by this woman who had been brought into Tall Moon's life . . . a woman he now knew he loved, even though they had only recently met.

It was Rowena's pure sweetness, her innocence, that drew Tall Moon to her, like a bee seeking pollen for survival.

Tall Moon had been in love only once in his life, to a woman who had died before he brought his Bird Clan to safety in Arkansas.

His wife's death had come at the hands of an evil white man who had found her alone by a stream on one of the nights when Tall Moon and his people had stopped to make camp. The white man had slit his beloved's throat and raped her.

Tall Moon had found the man kneeling over her, his pants still down at his knees, his wife's blood still dripping from the knife. It was only an instant later that this man's blood had mixed with his wife's, for Tall Moon had killed him immediately.

Tall Moon had buried his wife beside that beautiful stream, then had quickly led his people away from the area, fearing retaliation for his killing a white man.

Once they were finally settled in Arkansas, Tall Moon had made himself forget that horrible night, and what he had lost. Nothing could change what had happened, or the cruel fate that had brought that man to that stream at the very instant Tall Moon's wife had been kneeling over it, washing her lovely black hair.

Tall Moon had not loved any woman afterward, until now. He had to make certain that history did not repeat itself. He would not allow a woman he loved to be harmed by another white lunatic . . . even if that lunatic was his own brother.

Tall Moon did not feel anything but cold loathing for Darren. He knew now that sooner or later they would come to blows.

Chapter Twenty-one

As the lumberjacks ambled into the dining hall for breakfast, Rowena shifted nervously in her chair. Many of them were unshaven and dirty, hardly fit companions for a lady.

She had no appetite, whatsoever. She knew that she could force down neither eggs nor pancakes.

She just couldn't erase from her mind what she had seen last night: the poor roosters tearing each other apart, and then her violin smashed to bits.

Her precious violin, her only remaining memento of her past, was destroyed, and by a person she now feared was a madman.

She glanced quickly at Darren and felt cold inside when he gave her a devilish stare. He was waiting, no doubt, to see if she would keep her mouth shut.

She turned her eyes away. She didn't want him to see her fear and loathing. She didn't want him to know how profoundly he affected her.

She needed to get out of the dining room. She couldn't stand Darren's presence and the gawking stares from the men as they continued to come in and sit down to eat.

She had been at Lawrence's house for only two days, but already it had become unbearable.

"Are you all right, Rowena?" Lawrence's voice broke through Rowena's troubled thoughts.

She looked quickly at him, fearing that he might read her expression and guess that his youngest son had wronged her. She couldn't bear to be the cause of a fight between the two men.

"I'm a bit queasy this morning," Rowena finally said, forcing herself to keep eye contact with Lawrence, although she was afraid to do so might give him a glimpse inside her soul.

"What is causing it?" Lawrence asked, sliding a hand over and patting one of hers where it rested on top of the table. "Is it something you ate?"

"I'm not certain what is causing it, but I think I'd better not eat any breakfast," she said. "I would rather leave, Lawrence. I feel a ride on Misty might make me feel better. The morning air, and just being on Misty, always helps me feel better."

"Well, then, dear, you just go on and take that ride," Lawrence said. "And when you return, if you wish, I'll have Amos bring a bowl of soup to your room. Then perhaps you can nap away your queasiness if riding Misty hasn't done the job."

Rowena loved to see this gentle, caring side of Lawrence. So much of the time he was grumbling about this or that, or shouting out orders to the men working for him. When he was kind and considerate, he reminded Rowena of her father and how sweetly understanding and loving he had always been toward her.

She missed her father so much, her heart ached. If he were alive, he would be able to help her deal with her fear and anger.

But the fact was, if he were alive, she wouldn't ever have been put in this situation. Yet if she were still living in Georgia with her mother and father, she never would have met Tall Moon.

For the time being, she must find a way to tolerate the logging camp, because nearby was the man she loved with every beat of her heart. If she needed him, she knew that all she had to do was to go and tell him, and he would wrap her gently in his arms and help her.

"Thank you for being so understanding," Rowena murmured, glad to be able to escape Darren's prying eyes.

"You go now and enjoy your ride," Lawrence said, standing and helping her from her chair. "As I said, when you return, Amos will bring something comforting to your room, which for me is always a warm bowl of soup."

"That sounds good to me," Rowena replied, smiling into his eyes.

Rowena turned and hurried from the room, glad when she was finally outside. She hurried to the corral and mounted Misty, even though she wore a dress that was not made for riding.

It was a pretty, delicate thing, old, yet still one of her favorites. The dress was gathered at her waist, and the tiny purple flower design of violets, which had been hand-embroidered by one of the nuns at the convent, had been washed until they were so faded, she could hardly make out the flowers any longer.

Yet she still enjoyed wearing it. The high white collar hugged her throat, and the long sleeves kept the chill of the wind from her arms. The long skirt of the dress kept whipping up past her knees; she had to fight to hold it down so that her legs would not feel the coolness of this early morning.

Although it was spring, the nights were still cold enough to make a thick blanket necessary for sleeping.

Her long, golden hair fluttered down her back as she nudged Misty's sides, sending her into a faster lope. Both her cheeks and her eyes stung from the cool air rushing against them, but she reveled in the feeling of freedom.

She made her way through the forest, guiding Misty around tall oaks, and then finding herself riding beneath old elms, their bark curled up, their leaves fresh, new and green in the rays of sunshine spiraling through the foliage overhead.

She realized she had headed toward Tall Moon's village without even being conscious of it until now.

She drew rein and stopped. Gazing ahead, she saw that if she were to continue riding, she would find Tall Moon's village nestled beside the White River up ahead.

She badly wanted to go to Tall Moon and confide in him about what Darren had done to her violin. But she knew that she shouldn't.

He was already angry enough with his brother.

She would never forget the disgust in Tall Moon's eyes as he talked to her about the evils of cock-fighting.

He and Darren had tangled almost the minute they had realized they were brothers, brothers who held no love for each other in their hearts.

Yes, it was best that she didn't tell Tall Moon what Darren had done to her last night. She would have to carry that burden inside her heart, alone. She was afraid to tell either Tall Moon or Lawrence about the incident, for she believed that Darren was capable of killing both of them without blinking an eye.

She didn't want to be responsible for either Tall Moon's or Lawrence's death. If either one confronted Darren, she was afraid to think how he might react.

She rode on and on. Finally she felt herself relaxing and feeling somewhat better. Riding Misty always helped Rowena when she was unhappy. She could already feel the tension leaving her shoulders.

She inhaled a deep breath, loving the fresh scent of the forest. But a moment later, the putrid smell of death wrinkled her nose.

She gagged when she came upon a pile of dead roosters, some almost completely rotted, while others seemed to have just been thrown there.

Her thoughts returned to the horrible sight of the cockfighting arena, where men shouted at two roosters that were tearing each other apart.

She placed her hands over her ears, for she seemed to hear the men now, laughing and goading the roosters on. She could hear the pained squawks of the roosters as they each were torn by the sharpened spurs, and pecked by each other's beaks.

The last time she had looked, it seemed that one of the cocks had countless injuries around its neck, as though its head might be pecked clean off its body.

Looking down again at the pile of bodies, she gasped and felt faint when she saw that some of the roosters' heads were gone.

She swallowed hard and looked away again, her stomach rebelling at what she had seen. She was thankful she had not eaten anything since last evening, or she knew it would be coming up now.

"I must get out of here," she cried.

Just before turning Misty away, she stopped and gaped openly at one of the roosters. It had stirred, showing it had some life left in it.

Her heart pounding, she slid quickly from her saddle and bent low, even though doing so made her throat close up at the stench. Fighting back the urge to vomit, she reached out and started to pick up the rooster. Its eyes were now on her, watching her. She drew her hand quickly away when the rooster pecked at her.

Stepping back, Rowena wondered what she should do.

"I can't leave you there," she said.

The rooster's eyes still watched her as it lay bloody and limp amid the others. She stood there for a moment longer, wondering how she might manage to pickup the creature without being injured while doing so.

Then without further thought, she reached down, lifted the skirt of her dress, and ripped a portion of her petticoat off.

"Just behave long enough for me to wrap this around you," Rowena murmured as she again knelt down beside the pile of the roosters.

She tried not to breathe deeply as she reached out and finally managed to get the fabric around the injured rooster, holding him so that his beak could not reach her hands.

"Now what am I to do with you?" she wondered out loud.

She knew that she couldn't take the rooster back to the cabin with her. Its condition would be impossible to explain without bringing up Darren's cockfighting.

Her eyes brightened. "Tall Moon," she whispered.

Yes, she must go to him. Surely he would help the injured rooster, at least give the poor thing a chance at life again.

The rooster seemed too weak to fight back any longer. Its eyes were now closed. Rowena hoped it was just sleeping. Returning to her horse, she gently tucked the injured bird inside her travel bag.

This particular travel bag, which Lawrence had given to her for her use, was sewn into the side of the saddle. It was for carrying water and food, neither of which she had taken the time to bring with her today. There was plenty of room for the rooster.

"Now let's get you to Tall Moon's village," Rowena said.

She mounted Misty and rode in the direction of the village, hoping he would be there when she arrived, not out hunting with his warriors. She could not spend much time away from Lawrence's cabin. He was already worried about her. If she was gone too long, he might send Darren out to find her, as he had done yesterday.

She shuddered at the thought of being alone with Darren, then sank her heels into Misty's flanks.

When she finally saw the village up ahead, through a break in the trees, she smiled, knowing that she was moments away from being with Tall Moon again.

She now knew the meaning of passion, for that was what was awakened inside her at the thought of his nearness.

Chapter Twenty-two

Tears came to Rowena's eyes when she saw Tall Moon riding toward her. No doubt he'd been told by one of his warriors that she was coming.

"What has brought you here so early this morning, and alone?" Tall Moon asked as she drew rein beside his steed. "Has something happened that has frightened you?"

Rowena glanced down at the bag that hung from her saddle, and then at Tall Moon. "I came across something terrible while out riding today," she said, her voice drawn. "I have . . . brought . . . it to you. I hope you can help."

"What did you find? What have you brought?" Tall Moon asked, following the line of her vision as she again looked down at her travel bag. "What do you carry in your bag that puts such concern in your eyes and your voice?"

"I could not eat my breakfast because of what you and I saw last night, Tall Moon," Rowena said, swallowing hard. "I have always found solace on my mare, so I decided to take a ride this morning. While out riding, I came upon something so horrible, even now I feel sick because of it. I brought it to you, Tall Moon. It is in this bag, perhaps even dead by now."

Seeing that this was hard for her to talk about, and now curious, Tall Moon edged his horse closer to hers and reached out. But before he got the bag open, Rowena grabbed his hand.

"Be careful," she warned. "It pecks."

"Pecks?" Tall Moon repeated, his eyebrows lifting. "Are you saying that you have a bird in your bag?"

"A rooster," Rowena gulped out. "As I said earlier, I came upon a gruesome sight while riding Misty. It was a pile of discarded, rotting dead roosters, surely those that died during cockfights. Among them was this one . . . that . . . survived."

"And you picked it up and brought it to me?" Tall Moon asked, touched deeply by her caring heart. "It is here? In this bag?"

"Yes, but as I said, be careful," Rowena said, dropping her hand away from his. "It is quite angry, at least as angry as it can be in its weakened state."

Tall Moon carefully lifted the lid of the bag.

The rooster was no longer able to peck at him.

Its eyes were closed, and its head hung limply to one side.

"I think it is dead," he said, carefully sliding his hand inside the bag, then just as carefully easing it beneath the bird. Gently, he lifted the rooster from the bag.

"Is it?" Rowena blurted out, looking sadly at the bloody feathers of the rooster, and how limply its head hung in Tall Moon's hand.

"No, it still clings to life," Tall Moon said, seeing that the rooster was breathing. "Come with me. I will see what can be done for it. Then we'll place it in a coop by itself so that it can heal without others bothering it."

"I hope the poor thing lives," Rowena said as they both rode onward, soon entering the village where the Cherokee people were busy with their day's activities.

Most stopped and gazed at their chief and what he held. Then they looked at Rowena.

She couldn't read their expressions. They neither frowned nor smiled. It was as though they saw her, yet didn't.

It gave Rowena a strange feeling to think that Tall Moon's people were so indifferent toward her. She was so in love with him, and wanted to be with him forever. Would his people cause him to turn away from her?

Would he go that far to please his people? Would he turn his back on the one he loved, for Rowena believed that he did love her.

She had sensed almost the first moment they looked into each other's eyes that they had this connection.

She looked away from the villagers and rode onward with Tall Moon, stopping when he pulled up beside a round, thatched house that looked very different from the other dwellings in the village.

"This is the home of our people's Shaman," Tall Moon said, noticing that Rowena was looking curiously at the lodge. "His name is Good Spirit. He is a man who always uses his healing arts for the good of his people."

"Does that include injured . . . roosters?" Rowena asked as Tall Moon slid carefully from his saddle, the limp bird still held in one of his hands. "Will he know what to do to help it?"

"He knows all things," Tall Moon said, stepping up next to Rowena's mare as she slid out of the saddle. "He loves all things, whether animal, bird, or human. He will do what he can for the rooster. That is all that can be asked of him."

"The poor thing," Rowena again murmured.

"I won't be long," Tall Moon said, then stepped inside the conical-shaped lodge.

Rowena felt ill at ease standing there by herself. Once again, people stopped what they were doing to stare at her. Many looked at the Shaman's lodge, surely wondering why Tall Moon was there.

They must also wonder about the limp rooster that he had carried inside with him. Rowena hoped that the Shaman would agree to help the injured bird, and she hoped that he would make a quick decision about it. The longer she stood there, alone, the more Rowena felt like an intruder in these people's lives.

She knew they avoided white people, and there she was, white-skinned, and obviously someone their chief cared for.

She was very glad when Tall Moon stepped from the lodge, a contented smile on his face. "Good Spirit is already making medicine for the rooster and he assured me that he will make the creature well enough to live among others of its own kind again," he said.

He frowned as he turned and gazed at the closed entrance flap, then looked again into Rowena's eyes.

"I hope that this bird will not always want to kill other roosters," he said. "Once it is well, it would be sad if it did not know how to be with others of its kind. I hope this rooster will be able to put killing behind it."

"Where is the Shaman going to put the rooster while it recuperates from its wounds?" Rowena asked as she held the reins and walked her horse toward Tall Moon's corral.

"It will be kept separated from the others in a coop by itself," Tall Moon said, leading Magic inside the corral and placing him with the others there, while Rowena did the same with Misty.

"It is just so good that it is going to live after having been treated so horribly by Darren," Rowena murmured.

Tall Moon went to her and took her hands in his, gazing deep into her eyes. "You placed your steed with mine," he said thickly as he searched her eyes. "Does that mean you will stay for a while with me?"

The way that he was looking into her eyes, the way he held her hands, and the husky timbre in his voice, made Rowena's heart feel as though it were melting. This was a rapture she had only known after meeting Tall Moon.

"I . . . would . . . like to stay awhile before heading back to Lawrence's home," Rowena murmured, wondering what might transpire while they were alone together.

Surely he would do more than hold her. He would kiss her.

He might even do more than that if she allowed him to. And if she listened to her heart, she knew she would do anything he asked of her, for she wanted the same as he.

"Although we have not known each other for very long, you do know that I love you," Tall Moon said, searching her eyes with his. "You do know that I want to love and watch over you forever, do you not? If you would stay with me, instead of with my father, you know that I would protect you from all danger. I do not feel comfortable knowing that you are under the same roof as my demon brother. He is capable of anything. You know that. You have been around him long enough to understand."

"I believe that I understand better than anyone just what he is capable of doing," Rowena said, tears springing to her eyes as she again saw the splintered remains of her precious violin.

"What has he done?" Tall Moon asked, slowly removing his hands from hers. "I hear something in your voice and see it in the tears coming to your eyes. You have not told me everything that my brother has done."

A quick anger seized his insides. His eyes narrowed angrily. "He has not wrongly touched you, has he?" he asked, his voice drawn. "He has not come to your room in the night and—"

"No, it is nothing like that," Rowena said, wiping the tears from her eyes.

She looked from side to side, seeing how some people had stopped their activities again, to gaze at their chief and this white woman.

"Can we go inside your cabin?" Rowena blurted out, again gazing intently into Tall Moon's eyes. "I will be able to speak more freely there."

Almost afraid to hear what she was referring to, Tall Moon took Rowena gently by an elbow and ushered her inside his cabin. Once there, he closed the door, then turned to her and placed his hands on her shoulders as he gazed into her eyes again.

"Tell me," he said thickly. "What has my brother done that brought such hurt into your eyes?"

"I had thought it best not to tell you," Rowena said, lowering her eyes.

He placed a finger under her chin and lifted it, so that their eyes would meet again. "You can tell me anything," he said thickly. "Surely you know that. Why would you think otherwise, even for a moment."

"Because I know that what he did will enrage you as much as it hurt me," Rowena said softly. "I'm so afraid that if you confront Darren over this, he will find a way to kill you, maybe not right away, but when you least expect it. He is evil, Tall Moon, through and through. He is not one to turn your back on."

"My brother can never outwit me, so you do not have to worry about what he might try to do. He will not succeed," Tall Moon reassured her. "Tell me. What did he do?"

"He destroyed my violin," Rowena blurted out, new tears filling her eyes. "Of course you do not know about my violin, or how much it meant to me, but believe me, Tall Moon, it was the world to me. Out of all that I held dear to my heart before the war, my violin was the only thing that survived. My father sent me to a convent where I would be safe. All I took with me were some clothes . . . and my violin. And now it is gone! Darren broke it into a million pieces. It was a way to warn me against causing him problems. He knows now just how terrified I am of him. I am so afraid that he is plotting to kill Lawrence, and . . . and perhaps even you."

"Through the years I always wondered what my brother looked like and what sort of man he turned out to be," Tall Moon said, taking Rowena by the hand and leading her down to the soft mats on the floor before the fireplace. He placed an arm around her waist and drew her next to him, holding her tenderly close.

"And now you know," she murmured. "I'm sure you must be very disappointed to discover that he is nothing like you. Darren is filled with such hate it frightens me."

"I am sorry about your violin," Tall Moon said sympathetically. "I know it must have been very special to you."

"And now it is gone," Rowena said, a sob lodging inside her throat.

"If my brother had harmed you in any way . . ." Tall Moon took her hands and held them, then placed one over his heart. "Do you feel the thumping of my heart?" he asked, smiling.

"Yes," Rowena said, smiling back at him. "It is pounding quite hard. Why is that?"

"You know why," Tall Moon said, now taking that hand and kissing its palm. "I want you, Rowena. I have wanted you from the moment I realized that our destinies were fulfilled when we found each other."

"I . . . have . . . never been with a man before in the way that my body is telling me that I want you," Rowena said, blushing. She hoped she was not saying the wrong thing at the wrong time.

But, oh, how her body ached to have him.

This was all so new to her. She had never felt such sensual stirrings before. She knew that if he just touched her where her heart seemed to be centered at the juncture of her thighs, she would go up in flames.

She had been taught that a woman didn't give in to her need for a man until vows were spoken between them. But she wasn't sure she cared what the world thought anymore. Tall Moon now pressed her body down beneath his on the mats on the floor. He began to kiss her with such passion, she felt as though she might swoon from the wonders of his embrace.

As the kiss deepened, Rowena found herself straining up against his body with a hunger that was new to her. She was filled with overwhelming ecstasy as one of his hands crept up the inside of the skirt of her dress.

When he touched that place that no man had

touched before, stroking her where she felt strangely wet and wonderful, she started to push him away, but she found that she couldn't.

She wanted his hand there. She wanted to be caressed. His touch was causing all of her fears, woes, and sorrows to float away. They were being replaced inside her with a love so strong, she knew that what she was allowing him to do was right.

They were in love. They had found each other in a world that had gone mad and knew they were meant for each other.

She closed her eyes in ecstasy as his other hand went to one of her breasts and stroked it through the thin fabric of her dress.

Never in her life had she felt so needed, so loved. The warmth, the sweetness, coursing through her veins made her moan throatily.

"Do you want me to stop?" Tall Moon asked huskily, bringing her eyes open to gaze into his as his hands grew still on her body. "Or do you want me to make love to you?"

"I . . . I . . . need you so much," Rowena said, looking through glazed eyes into his. "I never knew what this need was that I had heard about, not until now. Oh, Tall Moon, do you see me as a brazen hussy because I allowed you—"

He brushed soft kisses across her lips, silencing the doubts that she was about to speak.

"I see you as a woman I will always love," he said, interrupting her. "I feel your love for me in everything you say and do. But if you wish to wait, I will stop now what I have begun."

"How can I ask you to stop, when everything

inside me cries out for more?" Rowena said, blushing at her openness with him. "Are you certain you will not see me differently once we make love? Will you still want . . . and . . . love me?"

"I shall always want and love you," Tall Moon said thickly. "I know what it is to love. Once I even had a wife, who was killed long ago. I loved her dearly, but it is different with you. I have never wanted a woman more than I want you. I have never loved anyone as much as I love you. I want you for my wife. I wish to marry you. Will you be my wife?"

"Are you certain?" she asked, searching his eyes. "We are so new to each other. Have you truly had time to know this is what you want? That it is I you wish to have as a wife?"

"I want nothing more than that," Tall Moon said, again brushing soft kisses across her lips. "Tell me that you will marry me. Tell me that you want to share lovemaking with me forever."

"I want all of that," Rowena said. "With every beat of my heart I want you, but what of your people? I am white. I know they will resent me."

"They want what I want, and if a wife with white skin is what fulfills their chief, that is what they want for their chief," Tall Moon said. "I have never wanted anything any more in my life than I want you."

"Oh, my darling, I feel the same toward you," Rowena said, then sucked in a deep, sudden breath of pleasure as Tall Moon kissed her passionately again. One of his hands stroked the juncture of her thighs as he prepared to introduce her to the ways of making love.

It all seemed to happen like magic—in no time they were undressed, their bodies warm against each other. Then Rowena felt something long and hard against her right thigh, and her breath caught, for she knew what it was.

It was the part of a man she had never seen before. It was the part of this man that would surely make her senses reel with pleasure.

He spoke softly against her lips as one of his hands continued to stroke her where she felt alive with building pleasure. His other hand was on one of her breasts, kneading it softly.

"There is a brief moment of pain, and then it will be all pleasure," he said huskily. "Relax. Enjoy. And know that I will always love you. Always."

He kissed her again and enfolded her within his arms, holding her gently as he slid himself inside her.

He heard her quick intake of breath as he delved more deeply inside her, and then gave one insistent shove that broke through the barrier of her virginity.

"The best is now to come," he whispered against her lips. "Let me show you. Let me teach you."

His lips came down onto hers again, and her blood surged in wild pleasure as he began his eager thrusts, each one sending her closer to the point of wondrous bliss.

Tall Moon had loved before, but nothing akin to how much he loved Rowena. His breath came in short gasps as the pleasure built within him with each added thrust.

He could not hold back much longer. The pleasure was turning to pain, his need for release was so urgent.

But he wanted her to feel it too. He could tell that she was awed by the intensity of her feelings. It was evident in the way she arched up against him, pure hunger in her demanding body.

Her body was trembling. She was clinging fiercely to him as she rode with him through each of his thrusts.

"My love, I cannot delay any longer," he said as he clung to her soft, creamy flesh. "My body . . ."

"Mine, too," Rowena found the breath to say. "What you are doing. I . . . I . . . never knew . . ."

"I will always love you," Tall Moon said, giving the final thrust that took them both over the brink of wondrous ecstasy.

Stunned by the intensity of what she had experienced, the beauty of their joining, the bliss that she had felt, Rowena lay there gazing at Tall Moon as he rolled away from her.

She reached out and ran a hand over his taut belly as he now lay on his back, his eyes peacefully closed.

She gazed at the part of him that had just taught her the miracle of sensual feelings, so deep she could still feel them within her. She knew that part of him had been much larger while he was making love, but now it lay limply relaxed against his thigh.

She wanted to touch it, but knew that she couldn't be that brazen. One day she would. She wanted to know all there was to know about the part of a man that had such command during lovemaking.

Suddenly Tall Moon reached down and took her hand. He turned on his side, facing her. "We must marry soon," he said thickly. "I do not want to think of you going back to that house where my brother lives. Stay. Never leave. Then I can be sure of your safety."

"But what about your father?" Rowena asked, also turning on her side so she faced him.

She could hardly believe that she was actually lying there, naked, with a man, and with such ease. But this was not just any man. This was the man that she loved with every fiber of her being, and a man she would soon marry.

"My father can take care of himself," Tall Moon said tightly. "Has he not done so for all of these years?"

"I believe things are different now," Rowena said, sitting up. She reached for her dress and slid it over her head. "Darren is more of a threat than your father realizes. I truly feel that I must return to your father's home. I am afraid for his life. Darren is capable of anything. He might kill Lawrence in order to gain full control of everything your father has."

Tall Moon stood up and slid into a breechclout, and then his moccasins. "Knowing that, you may be in the same danger as my father if you return to his home," he said, stroking his long, lean fingers through his hair, straightening out the tangles created by their lovemaking.

"Yes, I know that, but I still feel I should return to your father's cabin," Rowena said, standing. She straightened her own hair, so that it hung down her back, then tried to smooth the wrinkles from the skirt of her dress. "And there are the cockfights. Once your father hears of that activity, he will be sure to confront Darren."

"And what do you think you can do if he does?" Tall Moon asked, placing his hands on her waist and drawing her closer. "My woman, there is only so much you can do. Stay here where it is safe. Let me achieve what you want to accomplish."

He sighed, then said, "And as for the cockfights, I will take several warriors with me and we will steal the roosters that are still alive and destroy the cockfight arena and the cabin where the roosters are held."

"That would be too dangerous for your people," Rowena objected. "When Darren discovers what you have done, all hell will break loose. He might go to the authorities and make up some lie about you and your people and lead the cavalry to your home. They would send you to a reservation."

"I doubt my brother will go that far," Tall Moon said tightly. "I believe my brother took me seriously when I told him I would scalp him if he caused me any trouble. *Ho*, he is surely afraid of losing his red hair."

"I don't think that man is capable of being afraid of anything," Rowena said. "Please don't do anything that might bring harm to you or your people."

He drew her into his arms and gave her a gentle hug. "You worry too much. I am a man who has always been able to outwit any enemy that came my way," he said. "My brother is no different. I shall get the best of him."

They embraced again, then stepped outside. Quickly, they made their way to the corral.

Again he drew her to him and held her, then looked into her eyes. "It would be best if you stay," he said thickly. "There is nothing you need from my father's home, is there?"

"No, since I no longer have my violin to go for," she murmured. "But I still feel that I should return there. I must at least warn your father of the danger he is in, and say good-bye to him. There is no need for you to get involved. Your people need you. Think first of them."

"You are among those who are my concern," Tall Moon said thickly. "How can I let you go?"

"Because you should," Rowena said. She gave him a kiss, then mounted Misty. "I must admit I dread seeing Darren again, and being around him. I'm afraid I might do more than kick him this time if he gets in my way."

A slow smile crinkled the corners of Tall Moon's lips. "You kicked him?" he said, laughing softly.

She smiled and nodded.

He mounted his horse. "I will ride with you most of the way, then return to my village," he said, lifting his reins. "But think hard about returning here tonight. You are in danger. You know that."

"I know, but I shall be careful," she murmured. "I promise you that." She sighed. "I just know,

Tall Moon, that for now, this is what I should do. I owe your father this much since he was willing to give me a home."

"Just you keep an eye on Darren," Tall Moon said, riding from the corral.

"I wouldn't dare not to," Rowena said, glad to know that her days at Lawrence's house were numbered. Before long, she would most certainly return to Tall Moon, and stay with him, forever.

She could hardly wait to become his bride.

She could hardly wait to learn all of his people's ways so that they wouldn't be disappointed in their chief's decision to marry her!

Chapter Twenty-three

Rowena was glad that the evening meal was over. She had found it hard to sit there as though nothing was wrong.

She had felt Darren's eyes on her again all through the meal. It was as though he knew about her tryst with Tall Moon. But that was impossible.

She was in the study now, with both Lawrence and Darren. Both men were resting comfortably in plush leather chairs, smoking cigars, while Rowena sat, stiff-backed, on the sofa, facing the roaring fire in the hearth.

She felt the heat of her cheeks with her hands, wondering what was causing her blush. Was it her memory of the evening meal and the way Darren constantly eyed her? Or . . . was it what had transpired at Tall Moon's village, where she had made love with a man for the first time in her life?

Oh, how it made her heart race to think back to those moments when she was in Tall Moon's arms while he held her and kissed her as he taught her the true meaning of adoration and love.

Thoughts of their lovemaking lay so sweetly in her mind. Those recollections would help her through these next moments while she must sit with Darren and Lawrence and act as though nothing was different in her life.

Oh, if she could only have stayed with Tall Moon. He had asked her to.

The temptation had been so great, she had almost succumbed to his request, yet she knew that this was not the time to abandon Lawrence, not while his second-born showed such resentment toward him.

It was there now, the strain between these two men. She would catch an occasional glaring glance as Darren looked over at his father.

Both men were silent. She didn't understand why they spent the evening together when it was obvious they were not comfortable in each other's company.

She wondered how long this had gone on between them. Was their relationship always so strained?

Or had the strain begun recently, perhaps since they came to Arkansas to establish their lumber business? Had Darren wanted his father to do something else with the money that had been left after the war?

Rowena had no way of knowing. All she wanted was to know that she could leave soon to be with Tall Moon and know that Lawrence was not in danger of being harmed by his son.

"Well, my dear, what did this day hold for you while you were out riding?" Lawrence asked, suddenly breaking the silence in the room. "Do you feel safe traveling away from my home? Do you need someone to ride with you . . . perhaps Darren here?"

He gave Darren a sour glance. "You would offer her this service, wouldn't you, son?" he asked.

Then Lawrence laughed sarcastically as his eyes flashed into Darren's. "As though I'd even allow you to accompany her," he said tightly. "She's safer with a bear she might come upon in the forest than she would be with you, you son of a gun."

Lawrence grabbed his cigar from his mouth and leaned closer to Darren. "Hear me well, son, when I warn you not to do anything that might make Rowena feel uncomfortable," he growled out. "Do you understand?"

"I believe I do," Darren growled. He tossed his half-smoked cigar into the fireplace, rose, and started to leave. He stopped abruptly when he heard his father's next question.

"What do you think of my suggestion, Rowena?" Lawrence asked, tossing his own cigar into the fire. "Do you think you might do this for an old man? Would you go and get your violin and play me a song or two? We need something to break the tension that my son and I always seem to create when we are together."

He leaned back in his chair and got comfortable, smiling at Rowena as he waited for her to go get her violin. He saw no reason why she wouldn't play it for him. She had told him time and again how much she loved her music.

And now he was offering her an audience.

"Well? What are you waiting for?" Lawrence asked, raising an eyebrow and leaning forward as he stared at Rowena, who was behaving quite peculiarly. "Won't you play your violin for this tired old man?"

Rowena had grown pale at his suggestion. She glanced over at Darren, who stood there now, leaning nonchalantly against the door frame, watching her with a strange sort of amusement on his clean-shaven face.

Rowena's heart was pounding inside her chest. She felt trapped. She had no idea what to do, or what to say to Lawrence to explain why she wouldn't be playing her violin for him tonight, or any other night.

"I'm so sorry to disappoint you, Lawrence," she finally blurted out. "It has been such a long . . . tiring . . . day. I was just getting ready to ask you if it was all right for me to retire to my room. I've such a headache. Please understand."

Lawrence laughed good-naturedly. "Ah, sweetie, you're just bein' bashful," he said. "Come on, now. Go and get your violin. Playing it might even help you feel better."

"Damn it, Father, can't you see that she's serious about having a headache?" Darren spat out as he stepped farther into the room. "If she doesn't feel like playing her violin, she doesn't feel like playing it. Just leave her be, Father. Do you hear? Leave . . . her . . . be."

Lawrence glared at Darren. "Stop interfering in something that isn't your business," he growled out. "I know Rowena well enough now to realize that her violin gives her peace. She's said as much when we've discussed her music. It would be good for her to play it. It might even help her get rid of her headache."

Feeling more trapped by the minute, Rowena realized she was going to have to tell the truth. Lawrence was not going to let go of his suggestion that she play her violin. She got up and stepped between the two men.

She turned to Lawrence. Tears filled her eyes as she gazed down at him. "I can't play the violin, Lawrence," she murmured. "I just can't."

"Why not?" Lawrence asked, rising slowly from his chair. He went to her and put a gentle hand on her shoulder. "What's happened, honey? You can tell me."

"I don't have a violin any longer," Rowena blurted out, her spine stiffening when she heard Darren's gasp behind her.

She eased away from Lawrence's hand and turned slowly to gaze at Darren. She felt her insides turn to ice at the look Darren was giving her. If ever there was a look of hate in someone's eyes, she was seeing it tonight in Darren's.

Again she felt a hand on her shoulder as Lawrence turned her to face him again. "Where on earth is your violin?" he asked, his eyes questioning her.

"I'd . . . rather . . . not say," Rowena gulped out.

"Well, say it anyway, damn it," Lawrence shouted as he stepped away from her and threw his hand into the air in frustration. "Good Lord, Rowena, what in the hell is going on here? Where is your violin?"

When she still didn't answer him, and he caught

her looking over her shoulder at Darren, Lawrence stepped between them. Then he moved closer to Darren and spoke directly into his face. "What've you done?" he spat out. "Damn it all, son, what have you done to cause this tiny thing to look at you with such fear in her eyes? You'd better tell me, Darren, and if you did do something, by God, you'll feel my whip on your back the way you've never felt it before."

Darren glowered at Lawrence, doubled his hands into tight fists at his sides, then stomped from the room.

Stunned by his son's behavior, Lawrence stood there for a moment longer, staring at the empty space where Darren had just been. Then he turned and found Rowena collapsed into a chair, her face held in her hands as she sobbed.

Lawrence hurried to her. He bent to a knee before Rowena's chair.

He placed a finger beneath her chin and lifted it so that he could look into her face. "What's going on here, Rowena?" he asked thickly. "What aren't you telling me? What isn't Darren willing to say?"

"It is Darren," Rowena said between sobs. "He . . . he . . . broke my violin. It can't be repaired. He broke it into a million pieces of splintered wood."

"Why on earth . . . would . . . he do that?" Lawrence asked, stunned at her words.

When Rowena wouldn't answer him, but instead just looked back at him with a strange sort of fear in her eyes, Lawrence hurried to his feet.

As he left the room in a rush, he was already shouting Darren's name.

Rowena placed her hands over her ears, for Darren's name seemed to be echoing all around her. She could hear Lawrence out in the corridor, hurrying toward Darren's room.

Panic grabbed hold of Rowena. She knew that something terrible was about to happen. And she knew that it was because of her!

She shouldn't have told Lawrence what Darren had done. But Lawrence hadn't given her a choice. He had been so demanding.

Rowena leapt from the chair when she heard Lawrence and Darren shouting at each other. Then there was an ominous silence.

She was afraid to know what had caused it. She was afraid to stay in the house.

Tears almost blinding her, she rushed from the room. Minutes later, she had the saddle on Misty. But before she could leave, Lawrence was running toward her, shouting at her to stop.

She trembled as she waited for him to reach her. When he did, breathless from running, she was almost afraid to hear what he had to say.

"Things are all right, Rowena," Lawrence finally found the breath to say. "Darren and I worked everything out between us. It'll be all right. You see, I realize that I've been a mite too rough on my son, of late. He says I've been unreasonably harsh recently. I'm going to change. I want my son to be more comfortable in my presence."

He lowered his eyes, then looked at her again.

"And as for your violin," he said. "Darren said that was an accident. He said he saw it lying on your bed yesterday and went in to see what it felt like to play it. He told me he dropped it and when he turned to pick it up, he accidentally stepped on it. I'm sorry, Rowena. He's sorry. In fact, he told me he'd buy you another violin the next time he goes into town. That is, if he can find one in that dinky, tiny place."

Rowena was stunned by Lawrence's speech. How could he believe Darren's explanation about how he "accidentally" broke her violin.

But she wasn't about to say anything aloud to Lawrence. If, somehow, father and son could mend the rift between them, she couldn't be happier about it.

Perhaps it was even worth losing her violin.

"I'm so happy for you," Rowena said, giving Lawrence a gentle hug. "Now you and Darren can work together in peace."

But even as she was speaking, she feared that Lawrence had been fooled by a son who hated him and who was very good at lying.

"So you don't need to ride tonight after all, now, do you?" Lawrence asked, taking her horse's reins. "Remove the saddle, Rowena. Put Misty in her stall. Let's call it a night."

"Yes, let's," Rowena said, removing Misty's saddle as Lawrence stood, watching.

Then they walked together to the house, walked up the staircase, and retired to their own rooms.

Neither Rowena nor Lawrence had seen Darren standing in the darkness, his eyes filled with a seething hatred as he had watched his father go to his room and close the door behind him.

No one but Darren knew the truth . . . that his father would die soon.

His father would die tomorrow.

Chapter Twenty-four

Rowena had barely made it through breakfast and felt nothing but relief to be on Misty once again, heading toward Tall Moon's village.

She just didn't trust Darren's sudden acceptance of his father. She sensed that it was fake.

As she set off from their cabin, Darren had actually been walking with his father toward the lumber mill, with an arm around his Lawrence's shoulders, as though they were the best of buddies.

She had seen a look of joy on Lawrence's face, surely because he was so happy with the change in his son's attitude toward him.

"I just know it's fake," Rowena whispered to herself, a shiver riding her spine.

Usually she loved to ride through the forest, but this morning it seemed shadowed and eerie as she made her way toward Tall Moon's village.

With a foreboding sense of uneasiness, she sank her heels into the flanks of the mare, urging Misty faster as she reached a clearing where she could gallop. Her golden hair blew and fluttered in the wind. Her cheeks felt flushed from the rush of the early morning's damp wind against them.

"How can Lawrence be so blind?" she said aloud, into the wind.

But she knew Lawrence was blinded by the need to have a connection with his son again.

She wondered what Darren had said to make his father believe his lies so easily?

She realized that she would probably never know, but she did know one thing . . . Darren had cleverly turned his father's anger toward him over the violin into something strangely positive between them.

She swallowed hard when she recalled Lawrence and Darren walking together in the morning's sweet air, the sun warm on their smiling faces, as they walked toward the river.

Finally she saw Tall Moon's village through a break in the trees. She only hoped that he was there, and not out with his warriors on a hunt.

She rode onward, slowing the pace of her horse when she entered the outskirts of the village. Again she was aware of being watched as she passed by the villagers.

She ignored their stares and centered her attention on Tall Moon's cabin.

She was vastly relieved when he appeared from his cabin, just as she drew up in front of it.

"Rowena?" Tall Moon said as he came and helped her from Misty. "I can tell that something has happened. What is it?"

"I might be wrong, but I truly believe your father is in danger," Rowena said anxiously. "I have felt it before, but not the way I feel it today."

"Come inside and explain what you mean,"

Tall Moon said, ushering her inside his cabin where a fire burned softly in the fireplace.

He did not take her to the mats. Instead, as soon as they stepped inside, he turned her to face him. "Now tell me," he said thickly. "Why are you so alarmed about my *ah-te*? Did something happen?"

"It began last night," Rowena explained, encouraged by his mystically beautiful eyes gazing at her so lovingly. "After the evening meal, your father, Darren, and I retired to the study. I felt such tension between your father and Darren, even though they were sitting there comfortably in their chairs, smoking cigars."

"What happened?" Tall Moon asked. He took her hand and led her down onto the mats before the fire.

They sat facing each other as the fire's glow reflected in their eyes. "Your father asked me to play my violin," Rowena said. "I had to find a reason to refuse since I no longer had a violin to play, but nothing I said dissuaded him from wanting me to play. I felt terribly trapped, for your father was beginning to realize that something was wrong and Darren was standing there, waiting to see how I would explain to Lawrence why I couldn't play my violin."

"And what did you say?" Tall Moon asked, reaching a gentle hand to her face.

"I told him that I was so tired from the day's activities, and . . . that . . . I had a headache and wanted to retire to my room for the night," Rowena said softly. "But he wouldn't have it. He was determined that I was going to play for him. He tried laughing my reason off, saying that I was being bashful, but I think he was figuring out that something strange was going on."

"He didn't believe your reason for not playing your violin," Tall Moon said dryly. He leaned away from her and reached for a log, then placed it in the fire.

"No, he didn't believe it at all," Rowena murmured. "He looked at Darren and asked him to explain what he had done, for he obviously suspected that Darren was behind my reluctance to play."

She paused, then said, "It just all happened so fast. I blurted out that Darren had smashed my violin," Rowena said, swallowing hard. "I stayed in the study as they both left the room in a shouting match. And then I heard nothing but silence. I was afraid that perhaps one had hit the other. But . . . moments later Lawrence came to me, smiling. He said that Darren had told him about how he accidentally broke my violin, an explanation that Lawrence actually believed."

"And then what?" Tall Moon asked, searching her eyes.

She described what she had seen this morning, how father and son were walking together as though they were the best friends in the world, which was certainly not so.

"Do you believe that Darren is playing some sort of mind game with my father?" Tall Moon asked.

"I do," Rowena said. "Tall Moon, I truly believe your father is in danger. I'm afraid of what Darren might do to him. It's in Darren's eyes ... his need for total power, his hunger to possess what his father has. He wants it all so that he can be in control."

"Do you think Darren is capable of harming my father?" Tall Moon asked solemnly.

Rowena nodded, scrambling to her feet. "I think we should go there now and see if everything is all right. I have such an uneasy feeling, Tall Moon. Something is about to happen."

Tall Moon rose to his feet as well. He smiled as he framed her face between his hands. "So now the woman I love with all of my heart is having visions?" he said. "Do most white people have such powers?"

"Intuition," Rowena said, returning his smile. "I call it intuition." Her smile faded. "I hope my intuition, or vision, is wrong."

She grabbed his hand and urged him to leave his cabin. Then she took Misty from the corral and waited for Tall Moon to get Magic.

Without telling anyone where they were going, they left the village and hurried through the forest. They rode without talking until Tall Moon suddenly drew rein. Rowena stopped as well when she heard a loud noise. She flinched as she heard it again ... the crashing sound of a tree falling to the ground.

"The lumberjacks are now much too close to my village," Tall Moon said, his eyes meeting Rowena's.

She flinched again as the sound of another tree falling echoed through the thick forest. She could hear the men who were cutting the trees laughing and joking among themselves.

"I cannot wait any longer to make certain this is stopped," Tall Moon said tightly. "If I must take all of my warriors with me to my father's house, so be it. It must be done. Today, after I see that my father is all right, I will take him aside, and explain to him what he must do. My father must stop giving orders to saw the trees. It must stop today!"

"And if your father still doesn't listen to reason?" Rowena asked.

"He will be made to understand," Tall Moon said tightly.

Then he sighed heavily. "But first we must go and make certain that he is safe, that Darren has done nothing to hurt him," he said thickly. "There is too much about my *a-na-da-ni-ti* that is not right. Could he truly be evil enough to harm his own father? Surely not."

Rowena saw how Tall Moon was wrestling with his emotions as he tried to reason with himself about his brother. For herself, she had no need to pause and think about it. She was certain Darren was capable of harming his own father.

"We had better hurry on," she quickly said.

Chapter Twenty-five

The air was filled with the sound of lumber being sawed, and the smell of sawdust was thick as Tall Moon and Rowena rode out of the forest near Lawrence's cabin.

Rowena glanced at the cabin, wondering if Lawrence had gone back inside. The last time she had seen him he was arm in arm with Darren, walking toward the river and the shed where the lumber was prepared for shipping to St. Louis.

Tall Moon rode at a slower lope beside Rowena's mare, his eyes moving from place to place, searching out his father.

The activity was all happening inside the shed today, as no other lumber was arriving by river. But down at the shore he spotted a sudden movement. Rowena gasped when she, too, saw it . . . saw him!

"What on earth is Darren doing?" she asked as she glanced over at Tall Moon.

Darren was standing by the river's edge, clutching his father's lone arm. He was wrestling him to the ground.

"What does he think he's doing?" Rowena cried.

Tall Moon didn't respond. Instead, he sank his heels sharply into the flanks of his horse, and rode hard toward the river.

Rowena gasped as she saw Darren kick his father into the river, where several big logs floated in the water.

"Oh no," she cried, now riding hard to catch up with Tall Moon.

She saw Darren turn and stare in alarm at Rowena and Tall Moon riding hard in his direction.

"Stop!" Tall Moon shouted when Darren made a wide turn and began running toward the forest.

Neither Tall Moon nor Rowena watched him any longer, their main concern was for Lawrence. They knew that he couldn't survive for very long in the water. With only one arm, he couldn't swim.

"Oh no," Rowena cried when they got close enough to see him more clearly.

Lawrence had been shoved between two logs that were now drifting closer to him on both sides. Soon the current would push them so close, no one would be able to dive into the water to save Lawrence.

She now understood Darren's twisted plan. He had hoped that his father would be covered by those floating logs.

He had probably waited until all of the men were out of sight so that no one would see what he was doing, so that no one would know where to look for Lawrence when someone finally realized he was nowhere to be found.

Tall Moon slid from his saddle.

His eyes wide, his pulse racing, he ran to the

riverbank and fell to his knees beside the water, for there was no way he could dive in. The logs were now so close to Lawrence, no one could get in the river there. All that Tall Moon now saw of his father were his eyes staring back at Tall Moon as he began sinking, lower and lower.

Tall Moon looked desperately around him for help from the lumberjacks. But they were making so much noise preparing the logs that none of them had heard the commotion down by the river.

Rowena fell to her knees beside Tall Moon, her heart aching as she looked into Lawrence's eyes. His mouth, beneath the surface of the water, emitted large bubbles that popped and spread away into nothingness.

"Help!" Tall Moon shouted as he looked over his shoulder at the shed. "Someone! Come! Help!"

"I'll go for someone," Rowena gasped, scrambling to her feet. "They can bring something to move the logs apart."

"It . . . is . . . too late," Tall Moon said, his voice breaking as he looked into his father's eyes. A moment later his body went straight down into the river.

"Lord!" Rowena screamed as she, too, saw that Lawrence had disappeared in the water.

Several men had heard Rowena screaming. They stepped from the shed, eyes wide when they saw Rowena and Tall Moon on their knees, staring into the water.

Rowena looked at them as they ran up next to her.

"Lawrence is in the water there," Rowena cried, pointing. "Can you find a way to get those logs separated?"

Tall Moon's fingers were sore and bleeding from trying to move the logs so that he could dive in and retrieve his father's body.

When the two men shouted at Tall Moon to get out of the way, he stood up and stepped aside. The men took long poles and struggled and groaned as they began prying at the logs.

Soon the logs were separated enough so that Tall Moon had room to get in the water. Rowena watched him dive in and soon disappear from sight as he searched below for his father's body.

She grew afraid, for she saw that the men were finding it hard to keep the logs separated. If the space closed up again, Tall Moon wouldn't be able to get out.

In fact, he might even now be lost beneath those logs, unable to find the small space that was still left open.

"Please hurry, Tall Moon," Rowena cried, frantic at the thought of possibly losing him.

Oh, but she loved him so much.

And there was Lawrence.

How could Darren have done something so vicious, and to his own father?

If only she and Tall Moon had arrived at the riverbank a minute sooner. As it was, Darren had succeeded with his plan to rid himself of his father.

"Come on, Tall Moon," Rowena whispered to

herself, her eyes ever watching the water. "Please, oh, please, Tall Moon, make it back up before those logs—"

Suddenly Tall Moon's head popped to the surface. "Help get my father out of the water," he cried as he showed that he had his father by his one arm. He was hanging on to him for dear life as he looked from one log to another, realizing how close he had come to being lost beneath them.

The men were still holding the logs apart with their poles. Other men had joined them now, eager to help as they reached down and grabbed hold of Lawrence's arm, pulling him free. Another lumberjack reached in and helped Tall Moon out.

Rowena wanted to fling herself into Tall Moon's arms, so desperately happy was she that he had survived. But she saw that he had only one thing . . . one person . . . on his mind. He knelt now beside his father's limp body, then reached for Lawrence and ever so lovingly held him in his arms.

Rowena wiped tears from her eyes as she continued to watch son and father, touched deeply by the way Tall Moon continued to hold his father in his arms.

She knew that they had never expressed affection for each other, but still . . . this was Tall Moon's father, and he had died in the worst way possible . . . at the hands of one of his own sons.

She still couldn't believe that Darren could be so evil, and she now felt guilty for not having warned Lawrence about her earlier fears.

But of course Lawrence wouldn't have believed

her. What father would believe that his own son hated him so much that he would plot to kill him, and then actually do it?

Rowena felt such deep sadness over it all.

She stood there, watching, and then gazed into Tall Moon's eyes as he looked up at her. Gently, he lowered his father to the ground. He then rose to his feet and went to the lumberjacks.

He spoke to each of them, thanking them. Then he said something that made the men step away from him, their eyes wide with disbelief.

"You look at me as though you do not believe I have the power to tell you your work here is over. You will cut no more trees in this forest," Tall Moon said.

"You don't have the authority stop us," Lloyd Arden said, stepping up close to Tall Moon and glaring into his eyes. "Since Lawrence is dead, it is Darren's place to carry on for his father."

Tall Moon looked in the direction of where he had last seen Darren fleeing into the forest. His brother must realize that Tall Moon would not rest until he avenged his father's death.

Then Tall Moon looked Lloyd Arden directly in his eyes. "I am my father's oldest son," he said thickly. "I am in charge, now that my father is dead. And I say the lumbering operation is over along with my father's life."

"Darren will have something to say about that," Lloyd retorted, laughingly mockingly at Tall Moon.

"My brother Darren murdered my father," Tall Moon said, drawing gasps from the men, even Lloyd. "He is the one who wrestled him to the ground. He is the one who tossed him into the water between the logs. He knew that my father could not swim with only one arm. When he saw my arrival, he knew his game was over. He knew that his plan had just gone awry. He fled into the forest. He is hiding there now, but not for long. I shall find him. He will pay for the crime of murdering his own father."

He reached a hand out for Rowena. She took it and stepped close to his side. "Rowena saw it all," he said tightly. "She will confirm how my father died, and at whose hands."

Silence fell as the men slowly began backing away from Tall Moon and Rowena.

"All of you leave. There is no more money for you here. Do not think to question my authority," Tall Moon warned. "You do not want to even try to guess how you will be made to pay for going up against a powerful Cherokee chief such as myself."

Panic filled the eyes of all the men, even Lloyd Arden. They began running in every direction, quickly gathering their belongings before riding away on their horses.

Soon there was utter silence around Rowena and Tall Moon. They looked into each other's eyes, and then Tall Moon turned away from her and lifted his father's body into his arms.

Rowena walked with him as he went toward the cabin with his father.

"If you have any valuables in the house, you had best go now and get them," Tall Moon said. "I am taking my father inside to his bed, and then I am going to set fire to the cabin and everything that is in it. This house is going to be my father's funeral pyre."

Rowena was stunned at first by what he had planned, but knowing that Cherokee burial practices must be very different from hers or Lawrence's, she understood. Tall Moon would not want to give his father an Indian burial, for it had been obvious just how much his father detested everything Indian, with one exception . . . the Indian princess he had taken as his bride.

"I have nothing of importance in the cabin, just a few clothes," she murmured.

"When you become my wife, you will not need the clothes of a white woman, so just let them burn," he said. "Soon, my woman, we will marry and begin a new life."

"Your wife," Rowena said, thrilling at the very sound of it. She tired to think only of the happiness ahead, not how Lawrence had died, or Darren's part in his murder.

"*Ho*, you will be my wife, and as I have already promised, I will keep you safe from all harm, *I-gshi-di*, forevermore," he said thickly.

"I will be so proud to be your wife," Rowena said.

"Go and stand back from the cabin," Tall Moon said, nodding toward her. "I will take my father inside. I will say my final good-bye to him, then do what must be done."

Suddenly Amos opened the door and stared at Lawrence, lying limply in Tall Moon's arms. He turned his wide, questioning eyes to Tall Moon.

"Darren murdered him," Tall Moon said and

Amos gasped with shock. "It is true, Amos. Darren hated father enough . . . to . . . murder him."

"Where is Massa Darren now?" Amos asked, wiping tears from his eyes.

"He has fled in fear," Tall Moon said, going up the steps. "But he will not be able to hide for long. I will find him. He will pay for what he has done."

Amos stepped outside onto the porch, tears falling from his eyes as he looked at Lawrence.

"You get whatever things you want to take with you, for I am going to set the cabin afire," Tall Moon said, seeing shock enter the old man's eyes. "The house will be my father's grave."

"I see," Amos said, slowly nodding. "But what is to become of me?"

"You are welcome to go with me and Rowena to my village," Tall Moon said. "You can stay there for as long as you like. Forever, Amos, if you wish."

"Forever?" Amos repeated, again wiping tears from his eyes.

"The world is not a very safe place these days, Amos, not for you, or anyone," Tall Moon said. "I know of the plight of the black man. It is the same as that of the red man, even though President Lincoln spoke on your behalf and went to war to give you your freedom. But the reality is, Amos, your people are no more free now than before. They will always be looked down upon by whites, just as we red men are."

Amos glanced quickly at Rowena, then back at Tall Moon.

"Yes, Amos, her skin is white, but her heart

speaks the same language as mine," Tall Moon said. "She is going with me to my village. She will be my wife. You can go and be the free man you wished to be after the war. No one will be your master there."

"Amos, I urge you to go with us," Rowena said, as she reached a hand out for him. "Come with us now. I'm certain you don't have anything in that house you need to take with you. Let Tall Moon say his final good-bye to his father, and then we three will go to his village."

Amos nodded. "Yes'm," he said eagerly. "I want to go where you go." He left the porch and walked with Rowena far enough from the house so that the fire would not reach them.

Tall Moon carried his father's body inside and swiftly mounted the stairs. He knew not which bedroom was his father's, but it was enough to just place him on a bed. Any bed.

He chose the room and the bed and knelt down beside it. After saying a prayer, he left the bedroom and collected several lamps that were filled with kerosene. These he positioned throughout the house.

After lighting them all, he tossed each one to the floor so that the flames could spread rapidly through the cabin. Then he hurried outside and stood with Amos and Rowena, their eyes on the house as it was engulfed by fire.

Tall Moon turned to Rowena. "It is time now for me to hunt down Darren," he said, his eyes searching hers. "You can go to my village with Amos.

You can stay there until I find Darren and do what must be done."

"I want to go with you," Rowena blurted out. "I want to have a role in his comeuppance."

"Are you certain?" Tall Moon asked, again searching her eyes.

"Very," she murmured.

Amos's eyes were wide as he watched the fiery inferno of the house. He did not find it too hard to believe that Darren could be responsible for his father's death. Darren had slapped Amos around whenever he had taken the notion to. Amos had always seen him as the devil incarnate.

He could not help being glad that Darren would soon pay for all of the evil he had done. Amos smiled slowly at the realization that this Cherokee chief wouldn't allow Darren to harm anyone ever again.

Chapter Twenty-six

Birds flew from the limbs of the trees, scattering everywhere, as Darren ran blindly through the forest.

He was now in the midst of the cypress trees, stumbling in and out of the swampy mire. He was desperate to find a place to hide from his brother. His heart was pounding so hard, he could hardly get his breath, for he was afraid for his life.

Tall Moon knew what he was guilty of. It was something much worse than cockfighting. Yes, he . . . had . . . just killed his own father.

Stumbling and slipping, then steadying himself, over and over again, Darren ran onward.

He had not expected his brother to be anywhere near when he set his plan in motion.

Darren had forced himself to act as though he was his father's friend the prior evening, but only because he knew that after today, his father would never be able to ride him again over anything.

For a moment the night before, after Darren had explained the "accident" with the violin, Darren had thought maybe his father had chosen to change. His father had actually apologized to Darren for having ranted and raved at him.

But the next minute Darren had come to his senses. He'd realized that his father's kind behavior would only be short-lived, for it was not in his father to behave kindly toward Darren for very long.

His father was a tyrant who had always expected too much of him.

Darren's father had told him, time and again, that he was a big disappointment to him from the beginning. Darren would never be able to stand in his father's shoes or live up to his dreams.

Since Darren was old enough to act for himself, he had failed at most everything he had tried.

"Even this!" he cried into the wind.

No! He had not been able to kill his father without someone catching him in the act.

He had made certain that all of the loggers were busy away from the river so that he could be free to do as he wished there. Darren had even sent several of the men into the forest close to Tall Moon's village, though he knew that would enrage his brother.

How on earth had his brother known what he was up to? What had brought him to the logging camp at exactly the wrong moment?

And then there was Rowena! How on earth had she just happened to be with Tall Moon?

"How could they have known?" he again cried into the wind as he ran onward, still slipping and sliding in the mud beneath his feet.

It mattered no more why, or how, they knew. The fact remained that all Darren's plans had come to an abrupt end today. Instead of enjoying a life of leisure with his father's new wealth, he was running for his life.

Now Darren had nothing, for he could never return home again. All he actually owned were the clothes on his back.

He slapped the holstered pistol at his right side and ran his hand over the sheathed knife at his left, feeling fortunate that he had thought to arm himself this morning.

He had thought that if he was not able to push his father into the river, then by damn, Darren would have shot him dead, or stabbed him.

No matter what, Darren was determined not to live another day under his father's thumb. Yet now he was in worse straits than ever.

As he had so often done as a boy, hiding in a closet so that his father would not see him crying, he let tears flood his eyes at how much he had suddenly lost.

All of it.

He couldn't even watch his cocks fight anymore. They, too, were no longer his, for to retrieve them would be the same as walking into a trap.

"I've lost everything! Everything!" he cried aloud, his voice sounding strangled as it echoed back to him.

All that was left was his life, and even that might be short-lived if Tall Moon managed to find him.

Panic filled him. He must find a place to hide . . .
a place where neither Tall Moon nor Rowena could
find him.

It was only himself now against the world.

He stopped and wiped the sweat from his face
with the back of his shirtsleeve. He breathed hard
as he looked slowly around him.

He had never actually been this far from the
cabin. He wasn't sure just how close he might be to
the Indian village. But he knew a place that surely
was far enough from the village for him to escape
detection. He could hide there for a while, until
things cooled off a mite and he could find his way
into a town and try to start a new life.

But without a horse, he wondered just how far
he could get. He knew the dangers of this swamp.
He knew alligators lurked somewhere in these waters, and snakes could be upon you in the blink of
an eye, as well as spiders with their lethal bites.

Thus far, he had not seen any of those things.
Then his spine stiffened and he felt cold inside
when he heard the cry of a cougar coming from
somewhere in the distance.

Yes, it, too, was a danger to him. He had to get
on with finding a safe haven for himself.

He stumbled onward, making a sharp turn
right, toward the river, for he now knew where he
would go.

He remembered having seen several limestone
caverns in the area as he explored the river on rafts
with some of the lumberjacks. If he recalled accu-
rately enough, there were many caverns along the
river, high above the water level.

He was a skilled hunter. He wouldn't starve, and he would make bedding out of moss and the fluff from cattails. He could survive until he felt it was safe enough to flee elsewhere.

Almost too exhausted to put one foot ahead of the other, Darren ran onward, his lungs aching as he sucked in the putrid air of the swamp.

He was glad when he finally emerged onto solid ground, but here he faced a new torment. He was now walking through twisted blackberry thickets, and their briars ripped and tore at his breeches. They stabbed his flesh viciously.

Again he heard the cry of a cougar. It made goose bumps break out on his flesh, for the animal seemed closer. He had never seen a cougar in these parts, but . . . but . . . he had heard its cry more than once. He had always worried that it might find his cocks.

Now he had to worry about it finding him!

He pushed his way out of the treacherous thicket, stepping now onto a layer of soft, green moss. At last he could make good time, but his feet felt so heavy, it was as though he had stones tied to the bottoms of his shoes.

He panted.

He ran.

He shoved aside the low-hanging limbs of old oak trees, and then ran into a cobweb that made him shudder with fear as he found himself eye-to-eye with a large brown spider. He swung his arms and hands until he was free of the web, knocking the spider to the ground, where it crawled quickly in the opposite direction.

Darren began to run again, for up ahead he saw the limestone cavern that he had been searching for. It was only a short distance away.

He heard surging waters far down below him, where there was a small waterfall interrupting the steady flow of the river.

Panting hard, sweat pouring from his brow into his eyes, he finally reached the cavern. The ledge leading into it was dangerously narrow, but he felt he had no other choice.

Praying to himself that he would not slip, and that this was not the home of the cougar, Darren grabbed his pistol from its holster and held it steady before him. Carefully, slowly, he walked inside.

He stopped and took a deep breath as he looked around. In the depths of the cavern, he heard a slow trickling of water coming from some distant place. There was a smell of sour dampness.

He knew that this was a far different sort of place from what he was used to living in, but it would have to do. For now, anyhow.

With no sign of the cougar nearby, Darren set about getting settled in before night fell. He holstered his pistol and went outside to gather up a good supply of wood.

A short while later he had a fire started. He always carried a small supply of matches with him, in case of emergency.

He hurriedly made himself a place to rest, digging up the layers of soft moss that ran across the upper edge of the ledge. Later he would gather cattails down close to the river, and make himself a soft pillow from their fluff.

Then, he would have to hunt for his dinner. Tonight he would make it a silent kill, for he did not want to lead his brother to his hiding place.

In a few days, he expected that he would no longer be the hunted, and his brother would assume he had left the area.

He gazed down at his pistol. He grimaced when he suddenly realized just how few bullets he had with him.

But he had never expected to flee the camp so abruptly. He had thought he would be set for life once his father's body disappeared in the river.

Yes, he must use those few bullets wisely. He only hoped he would get the chance to use one on Tall Moon, and another on Rowena.

Nothing would please him more than to know they were out of his way forever.

He might have a semblance of peace inside his heart to know that he never had to watch over his shoulder for the rest of his life, for chance one or the other might be there, to kill him.

He sat down on the moss, too tired at this moment to try to find something for his supper.

Although he felt safe enough for now, he felt a strange gnawing emptiness inside that had nothing to do with being hungry. He had never before been without his father's guidance.

He wondered if his father's spirit would haunt him? He didn't believe in ghosts, yet he had heard that the Cherokee believed in all sorts of superstitions like that. In this wild land where the Cherokee had established their homes, it was easy to believe in such things.

He looked slowly around him, then turned and peered farther into the blackness of the cavern, a sudden shiver riding his spine.

Chapter Twenty-seven

The sky was turning orange from the fiery inferno as the cabin burned. Smoke mingled with the flames, causing Rowena to draw farther away.

She gave Tall Moon a frightened look.

"Surely someone will see the glow of the fire and the black smoke billowing into the sky," she gasped, her eyes wide. "Might that not draw more white people here?"

"The nearest town, Jasper, is quite a distance away," Tall Moon said reassuringly. He heard the fear in her voice and saw it in her eyes. "No one from there would be able to see the smoke and flames, and there are no established homes anywhere near here. My *ah-te* was the only one to settle here after my Cherokee people."

She looked over at Amos, who was also watching the burning cabin.

She could see that he was trembling. He had already suffered so many horrors in his life, she wished she could spare him yet another upheaval.

She went to him and gave him a gentle hug. "Tall Moon said we had nothing to worry about," she murmured. "That includes you."

Tall Moon went to them and with his muscled arms embraced them both. "You both are safe," he said calmly.

He stepped away from them. "Amos, will you come with Rowena and me?" he asked. "No one will ever bother you at my village."

"I've been thinking," Amos said. "I need to find my own way in the world now. I need to find some of my own people. I only stayed with Massa Lawrence for as long as I did because I saw how he needed me. But now that he is gone from this earth, I have needs of my own. I am lonely for those of my own kind."

"Amos, do you have any idea where to go?" Rowena asked softly, understanding his need to move on with his life.

He had given of himself to white people long enough. It was time for him to think of himself and his own future. He was such a kind and loving man, she hoped that he did not fall on hard times while seeking his happiness.

"I don' need any particular direction," Amos said, slowly smiling. "I will just go until I know I'se where I'se 'sposed to be."

Tall Moon looked toward the corral and saw two horses. He recognized the one horse as being his father's and assumed the other belonged to his brother.

Although he guessed that his father had not been able to ride well since he'd lost his arm, he had kept his horse anyway. Perhaps it reminded him of what he had once been before the war.

The horse had been his father's ever since Tall

Moon had been called by the name Thomas and lived with his beautiful mother in the huge white plantation house. Tall Moon knew the love his father had had for that horse. It was on that very horse that he had taught Tall Moon how to ride.

Tall Moon felt a sad regret when he remembered those days. For a short time his father had actually treated him like a son.

Although Tall Moon loved horses with a passion, and would enjoy keeping the steed that had been his father's, he felt that he must let go of everything that belonged to his past.

And who better to help him put that past behind him than Amos, whose own past had been taken from him?

He turned to Amos. "Come with me," he said, throwing a smile at Rowena, who was watching him. "I will give you my father's horse. It is yours now for as long as you wish to have it. Perhaps on this horse you can find what will be your future."

"You gonna give Amos that horse?" Amos asked, his eyes wide as he walked between Tall Moon and Rowena to the corral. "Both of these horses are such fine animals." He looked at Tall Moon again. "You want me to have this fine horse, to keep as my own?"

"Like I said, Amos, it is yours for as long as you wish it to be. Take the other one as well, in case you need to rest one while you ride," Tall Moon said, entering the corral. He had no saddle to put on the steed, so he hoped Amos knew how to ride bareback.

He patted the horse's neck and put on its bridle.

It was a beautiful strawberry roan, with only some white whiskers around its nose showing its age. Otherwise, it was still muscled and fine looking, its dark eyes meeting Amos's as he stepped up and stroked its withers.

"Mine? Truly mine?" Amos asked, turning wide eyes to Tall Moon again. "Are you certain? You want ol' Amos to have such a fine horse as this for his own?" He looked over at the other one, which was a lovely brown mare.

"They both are yours." Tall Moon said, giving Rowena a smile. There were tears in her eyes. She knew that this black man had never owned much of anything that he could call his own. She was touched by his joy in receiving something as grand as these horses.

She wiped the tears from her eyes and watched as Amos got on the strawberry roan. He looked a little uneasy, since it had surely been a long time since he was on a horse.

"You can ride it, can't you?" Rowena blurted out.

"Yes'm, I can," he said, just as he slid to one side when the horse took a step toward the open corral gate.

"Brace yourself with your knees," Tall Moon said, stepping aside as Amos managed to ride out of the corral. His eyes were wide as he smiled from Rowena to Tall Moon.

"I can do it," Amos said with a relieved smile.

"Just take your time," Tall Moon instructed, walking alongside the horse for a short distance. "Think about how this horse is taking you to places you have never been before and you will be able to ride it for as long as you want to ride."

"Yassuh, for as long as ol' Amos wants to ride," Amos repeated. He rode away from Rowena and Tall Moon for a short distance, then stopped when he saw Tall Moon coming to him with the lead rope of the other horse in his hand.

"Take this second horse with you, too," Tall Moon said, handing Amos the rope. "Take turns riding them. That way neither will get too tired."

"Yassuh, I will, and again, thank you," Amos said.

"Now go on and find your new life," Tall Moon said, affectionately patting the rump of his father's steed. "May the Great Spirit guide your way."

Amos smiled a little awkwardly, nodded, then rode away. Before he disappeared down the road he paused to look over his shoulder and smile one of the brightest smiles Rowena had ever seen.

"Take care, Amos!" she shouted.

"I will, Miss Rowena," Amos shouted back over his shoulder. "I will. And thank you!"

They watched him until Amos and both horses disappeared around a bend in the road.

"He will be all right," Tall Moon said, turning to Rowena and drawing her into his embrace. "And so will you. Soon you will be my wife, and I will be your husband. But first we must find my brother and make him pay for the evil he has done."

"But he has been gone for so long now, how can you find him?" Rowena asked, searching his eyes.

"We Cherokee are skilled at tracking people,"

Tall Moon replied. "That is how I will find my brother."

"You can actually do that?" Rowena asked, arching an eyebrow. "I have heard that Indians are expert trackers, but I didn't think that I would ever witness such a thing."

"You will today see how it is done," Tall Moon said as he stepped away from her. They went back to where they had last seen Darren, just before he ran into the darkness of the forest. "I will begin looking for footsteps that show one shoe larger than the other."

"What do you mean?" Rowena asked, watching how he intently surveyed the ground. "Why would you look for something like that?"

"From the first time I met my grown brother, I noticed that his footprints were uneven," Tall Moon explained. "He was born not only with a twisted, evil, greedy mind, but also with faulty feet."

"My word," Rowena said, placing a hand at her throat. "I never would have noticed."

"Only someone who studies footprints would," Tall Moon said. "I am examining the earth now, to see which way my brother went. We both know that he didn't stop to take his horse. He was in too big a hurry to think logically. He just acted on instinct and ran."

Tall Moon's eyes carefully searched the earth. There were many footprints made by the men who had worked there.

But one set of prints went in a different direction from the others. The lumberjacks had gone to get their belongings or to the corral to collect their steeds before riding away at Tall Moon's command.

This one set of prints led into the forest. Tall Moon smiled smugly.

"These are my brother's," he said, smiling over his shoulder at Rowena.

He then went to her and took her gently by the elbow. He ushered her to her horse and helped her into the saddle.

"You are certain you've found Darren's footprints?" Rowena asked as Tall Moon quickly mounted Magic.

"I have no doubt, whatsoever, that these prints are his. I noticed that one foot is larger that the other," Tall Moon said, bringing his steed up close to hers. "Are you ready? Are you ready to track down a murdering scoundrel?"

"Yes," Rowena said determinedly.

They rode off together into the forest, riding slowly as they followed the footprints that were so visible to Tall Moon's eyes, yet were scarcely noticeable to Rowena's. She found it absolutely incredible that he could actually see the prints and keep following them.

Suddenly Tall Moon brought his horse to a stop. Darren's footprints had disappeared into the swamp.

Tall Moon smiled with relief when upon closer observation he found Darren's prints where they came out of the swamp and went onward again.

"I know where my brother is going," Tall Moon suddenly blurted out.

"Where?" Rowena asked, moving her mount closer to Tall Moon's.

"He is going to hide in one of the limestone caverns that are visible to those boating on the river."

"But if you guessed where he might be so easily, wouldn't you think that Darren would realize the caverns are not a good place to hide?" Rowena murmured.

"My brother does not seem to be thinking things through very carefully," Tall Moon said thickly. "When he killed our father, do you think he was thinking logically then?"

"Most certainly not," Rowena said.

"I just know he has gone to one of the caverns," Tall Moon said. "His footprints will tell us which one."

The prints led them into dense stands of cypress elms and green, mosquito-laden swampland, but determined to find his brother, Tall Moon urged Rowena to ride onward with him.

He was on a mission. Nothing could stop him.

He was going to make certain that his brother got his comeuppance for the evil he had done, not only to his father, but to almost every creature around him.

He thought about the roosters that stood in a pen even now awaiting their next fight to the death. That was never to be, for Tall Moon was going to rescue them and tame them.

Rowena swatted constantly at the mosquitoes, already feeling the itch from their bites. But she was as determined as Tall Moon to find Darren and see justice done.

What were a few mosquito bites compared to the wrong he had inflicted on his father, and the wrong he might yet do if he wasn't stopped.

Chapter Twenty-eight

His horse tethered close by, Lloyd Arden crept through the thick foliage toward the small cabin that housed the roosters. He glanced at his friend Adam, glad the other man was with him.

"We're takin' a chance at gettin' scalped," Adam grumbled as he followed Lloyd. He looked nervously from side to side, and over his shoulder, to see if they were still alone. "That damn savage meant business, Lloyd. He told everyone to scat, yet here I am, stupidly going against what he said to do, chancing losing my life to help you save a couple of damn roosters."

"They're mine," Lloyd argued. "And they're worth a lot of money."

"Worth losin' our lives?" Adam growled. He nervously ran his fingers through his thick black beard. "I wonder if they scalp the hair off a person's face after takin' it from his head?"

Lloyd stopped quickly and turned to Adam.

He glowered at him. "You've been promised half the pay the cock makes for me at the next fight. So . . . shut up, Adam. I don't need your constant fussin'," he said. "We both watched the black man ride away in one direction, and the savage and the woman in the other. They're all long gone. From what I could tell by the savage's behavior, he's trackin' good ol' Darren. He's out for blood. And it's not ours he wants. He's after the one he now claims as his brother."

"How on earth could that be?" Adam asked, raising an eyebrow as he hurried alongside Lloyd again. They were now close enough to see the fence that enclosed the arena. "Darren never mentioned havin' a brother, much less him bein' red-skinned."

"Now, would you admit to havin' such a brother, if you had one with that color skin?" Lloyd asked, snickering. "Both Darren and his pa had quite a skeleton hid in their closet, wouldn't you say?"

"I wished he'd stayed there is all that I've got to say about it," Adam grumbled, almost beneath his breath. "Lloyd, let's get those roosters and hightail it outta here as fast as we can. I'm hankerin' for some clean air that doesn't carry the savage's stink in it."

"You'd better watch your mouth. That Injun might be where he can hear you," Lloyd said, grinning wickedly at Adam. "But say it again. I liked the sound of it."

Adam laughed, then grew somber again when they reached the fence. Without saying anything else, they both entered the arena, then went on into the cabin.

The stench was almost unbearable, and they both quickly covered their noses with their hands.

One of the roosters, one of Darren's, had died. The others squawked fiercely as they paced in their own droppings in the tiny cages.

"Good Lord in heaven," Adam gasped. "Just look at this place. Are you certain you want to take those filthy birds with you?"

"Those filthy birds, as you call them, will be makin' us top dollar when we get to the next cockfight," Lloyd said, already walking toward the four cages that housed his roosters. "I've heard of a place not far from Jasper, where there are some mighty good fights goin' on once or twice a week. That's where we'll make our money," he said, looking over at Adam, who still seemed stunned by the filth surrounding him.

"Snap out of it, Adam," Lloyd said sternly. "You grab those two cages over there, whilst I grab these others."

"So you're only taking yours?" Adam asked, hurrying to the two cages that Lloyd had pointed out to him.

"We don't have a way to transport any more than that," Lloyd said. "It's going to be mighty awkward as it is, carrying those cages at the sides of our horses. But I'll grab a good bit of rope to tie 'em on. It'll be just fine, Adam. Just fine."

"I cain't wait to put many a mile between myself and that Injun," Adam said as he grabbed two cages. He almost gagged, the smell was so intense, especially now that he couldn't cover his nose and mouth with his hands.

"You know that Cherokee village ain't so far

away," Adam grumbled. "I'd hate to have one of those warriors catch us this close to their home after the one redskin ordered us away."

"Just have faith, Adam, just have faith," Lloyd said, eyeing the two roosters in the cages he was going to carry on his own horse.

He saw a certain listlessness in their eyes and supposed it was from hunger and lack of water. He could tend to feeding them now, but watering would have to come later.

He went to a tall container, where the chicken feed was stored.

After grabbing a handful, he went to his roosters and tossed some into each cage, and then did the same for the roosters in the cages that Adam was holding.

"Come on, Lloyd, let's get the hell outta here," Adam growled. "We don't really know how far the Injun went. He might backtrack, even. What if he catches us doin' what we know we shouldn't be doin'? The Injun's threat made me almost wet my breeches."

"No one, not even a fierce Indian, is going to take my roosters away from me," Lloyd said, picking up each cage by the handle and walking past Adam.

He nodded toward his friend. "Come on," he said tightly. "I thought you were the one anxious to leave."

"I am, but I can't help thinkin' the Injun might be watchin' our every move. Maybe even now he's holding his knife ready to scalp us," Adam said.

He shuddered with fear. "Those roosters might squawk as we travel, drawing attention we just don't want."

"Had I known you were such a scaredy-cat, I'd have chosen someone else to help me rescue my cocks," Lloyd said, giving Adam a sour glance. "Come on. Stop your squawkin', or I'll put you in the next cockfight arena we come to. We'll just see what you say when you have to fight off those son of a guns."

"You wouldn't . . ." Adam said.

"Naw, just jestin'," Lloyd laughed. "But I do wish you'd stop fussin' like a frightened schoolgirl who's afraid of a boy lookin' at her."

They ran to their horses, which they had tethered beneath a tall, old oak tree.

They both said nothing else as they tied the cages on each side of their steeds, secured by knots to the saddle.

"They're in for quite a ride, wouldn't you say?" Lloyd commented as he stood back and noticed the roosters trying to keep their feet in the tilting cages. He swung up into his saddle. "Come on, Adam. We've been in these parts long enough."

He smiled as he waited for Adam to mount his steed. "The other roosters can rot as far as I'm concerned. Something tells me that nobody will come to their rescue," he said, snapping his reins and riding off beside Adam. "The other lumberjacks have all hightailed it out of here. And I doubt the Injun knows about them the roosters. No. Those poor cocks will die of neglect trapped in their cages."

"It's a shame we couldn't take them all," Adam said. "I could've taken Darren's as mine."

"We don't have room for any more than we're carrying now," Lloyd said tightly. "So quit thinkin' on the impossible, Adam. Do you hear?"

"We could come back for the others later," Adam persisted. "Want to give it a try after we get these four settled in somewheres in a pen?"

"I wouldn't try comin' back here if someone were to pay me top dollar to do it," Lloyd said flatly. "I've risked my neck to get these four. I ain't riskin' it to get the others."

They rode quickly through the forest, the shine of the river at their left side. They rode farther and farther from the lumber camp, the roosters squawking frantically at each bounce.

"Shut up, you stupid fools," Lloyd grumbled as he looked over his shoulder.

"I've got the most horrible feeling of bein' watched," Adam said, shivering. "Do you feel the same?"

"You dumb bumpkin, don't you know it's only the wind?" Lloyd said, then again looked ahead of him, truly hoping that was their only company. This was not the day he wanted to die.

Chapter Twenty-nine

The sound of water splashing over rock made Tall Moon realize that they were close to the caverns where he suspected Darren was hiding.

He recalled a waterfall near one particular cavern. He also remembered how narrow was the ledge approaching that cavern.

He had one day thought of investigating it after picking blackberries close to the cavern. But when he had seen how sheer the drop-off was, and that it would take only one misstep to plummet down to the river, he had thought it wasn't worth the risk. He had picked the berries and returned home.

It was ironic just how close to his village this cavern was. Not even a mile away, his people would be preparing for the night.

He reached out a hand to Rowena. "Stop," he said, only loud enough for her to hear. He nodded toward the cavern. "My brother is there."

When the wind suddenly shifted, his nose picked up the smell of meat cooking over an outdoor fire. He knew where the fire and the scent of the meat came from. His brother had felt confident enough to hunt near this cavern and even build a fire.

He had not known his brother Tall Moon well enough to be aware of his skill at tracking, or Darren would have been more careful than to build a fire.

"Rowena, dismount," Tall Moon said, sliding from his saddle. "Secure Misty's reins to a tree, and then come with me."

Rowena nodded and did as he commanded, then went to him and walked stealthily at his side. They made no sounds as they stepped over fallen limbs and through the leaves.

When they got a few feet farther, a break in the trees afforded them a good look at the cavern as well as the campfire. A rabbit was cooking over it, the meat dripping its juices into the flames.

"Surely it isn't Darren who built this fire," Rowena whispered to Tall Moon. "Surely he would know that someone might be near enough to smell the smoke and come to investigate."

"My brother is not of the same world I grew up in, so he would not think of these possibilities," Tall Moon replied softly. "He has never had to be cautious, or to guard his own safety and well-being. He always had my father to do this for him."

"What are you going to do now?" Rowena asked as she gazed at the knife sheathed at his waist.

He did not have his bow and arrow to use today. Only the knife.

If Darren had brought a firearm with him, he

would have both Tall Moon and Rowena at a disadvantage.

"We will approach my brother and tell him that he must give himself up," Tall Moon said thickly. "He has committed a horrendous crime. He cannot be allowed to continue his wrongdoing."

"But what are you going to do if he refuses to give himself up?" Rowena asked, searching Tall Moon's eyes as he turned to her. "If he killed his own father, he will not bat an eye over killing you or me."

"We will only know the depth of his hatred for me when I show myself to him," Tall Moon said. "I want you to stay hidden. He does not need to know that you are here. If things go awry and he manages to get the best of me, run away. Run far away. Go to my village." He nodded in the direction of the Cherokee village. "Tell my people what has happened. They will take care of everything else."

"I think you should go to your village and get several warriors. Together you can return and surround your brother," Rowena said, touching her hand to Tall Moon's arm. "Don't give him a chance to kill you. Why would you take such a risk?"

"I hope there is some measure of sanity left in my brother," Tall Moon said, his voice drawn. "I hope that he regrets the murder he has committed and will allow his brother to approach."

"But don't you see?" Rowena softly pleaded. "He has never seen you as a brother. You are nothing but a stranger to him."

"I must do this in the way I see best," Tall

Moon said, taking her hand from his arm. He kissed its palm, then dropped it to her side.

He turned quickly toward the cavern when he heard movement. His eyes widened when he saw Darren ease his way across the narrow ledge to check the meat that he was cooking on the fire.

He saw that Darren wore no weapons at all. If he had had any, he had surely taken them off and left them in the cavern.

Obviously, Darren was certain no one would find him. That was the mistake Tall Moon needed. He knew now that Darren's capture would be possible.

At that moment Darren let out a loud cry for help. Tall Moon and Rowena stared disbelievingly at Darren as he lost his balance on the slippery ledge and fell, catching hold of the rocky edge.

He was clinging for his life, his eyes wild as he looked from side to side, and then below.

Tall Moon leapt out into the open. He ran to the ledge.

As Rowena watched in disbelief, she saw Tall Moon risk his own life for his devilish brother. He reached down and grabbed both of Darren's arms, even though he, himself, was in danger of falling, too. The ledge was so narrow, it was hard for him to stoop without falling over the side as well.

But he managed somehow to hold on to Darren, then slowly pull him up, to safety.

Rowena's heart was pounding so hard, her knees had grown weak. She expected Darren to reach up at any moment now and grab Tall Moon, yanking him over the side to his death, even though to do so would mean his own death as well.

But to her relief, Darren hung on to Tall Moon's arms for dear life, and soon they were both away from the ledge and stretched out beside the fire on their backs, panting hard, as they stared into the blue heavens.

"Why . . . did . . . you save . . . me?" Darren finally asked as he looked over at Tall Moon. "Why didn't you let me fall? Or . . . do you have even worse plans for me? What are you going to do with me, Tall Moon? What sort of punishment do Indians have for those who have wronged others?"

Rowena moved slowly toward them. She was so relieved that the man she loved had not fallen to his death. She fell to her knees beside Tall Moon and took one of his hands in hers.

Darren gasped as he looked her square in the eye.

"You," he said, his voice dry.

"Yes, I came with Tall Moon to find you," Rowena said as Tall Moon sat up and drew her into his arms. "How could you have killed your very own father, Darren? How could you have hated him so much?"

Darren said nothing, only turned his eyes away.

"Oh Lord, Tall Moon, you could have died," Rowena exclaimed, as she clung to him. "You came so close. . . ."

She swallowed hard. "I came so close to losing you, forever," she cried, sobbing.

"The Great Spirit has more things for me to do

on this earth before I die, so I was saved for that reason," Tall Moon said.

Rowena glanced at Darren, who had turned away from them both. "But to risk your life, when you have so many people depending on you, to save . . . that . . . demon?" she said, shivering.

"It is over, so do not think anymore about it," Tall Moon said, looking at Darren, who had curled in a tight ball on his left side.

"But . . . what . . . of him . . . now?" Rowena had to ask. "Are you going to take him to the white authorities?"

"No, that is not my plan," Tall Moon answered.

"You have a plan?" Rowena asked.

"I have a plan," Tall Moon said, nodding.

"Is he going . . . to . . . die?" Rowena asked, rising to her feet with Tall Moon's help.

"It was never my plan to kill him," Tall Moon said, placing his hands on her waist and gazing directly into her eyes.

"Then what are you going to do?" Rowena asked, stunned at Tall Moon's ability to tolerate this man who was so evil.

"My brother has never claimed the side of himself that is Indian," Tall Moon said, glancing over at his brother, who still lay lifelessly staring away from him and Rowena. "I believe the worst punishment of all for him would be to have to live among the Cherokee and live the life of a Cherokee."

"What?" Rowena gasped, her eyes widening. "Are you saying he will be free to roam among your people, and do as he pleases?"

"I did not say that," Tall Moon said, slowly smiling. "He will live among my people, but he will be guarded. Every move he makes will be watched until . . ."

"Until . . . ?" Rowena asked, amazed that this man could be so generous to someone who had proven his hate for not only his father, but also Tall Moon.

"Until he proves that he has recognized the Indian side of himself and respects it in all ways," Tall Moon said, now walking away from Rowena. He went to Darren and knelt beside him, so that Darren was forced to look at him.

"Did you hear what I said?" Tall Moon asked. He placed a hand on his brother's arm, forcing him to a sitting position. "You are going home, my brother. *My* home. You will live life as you have never known it. You will live the life of a Cherokee! You will learn in all ways how to become Cherokee. You will not be able to back down and refuse to do anything that is expected of you, or you will be locked away in a dark cabin, without food or water until you decide to cooperate again. In time, you will soften. In time you will regret having taken your father's life. You will pay for your misdeed by feeling the pain of his loss every day. He was not the most perfect father, but he was . . . *your* father . . . my . . . father."

"I can't do any such thing," Darren finally said, looking squarely in Tall Moon's dark eyes. "I refuse. I would rather die than become . . . as . . . you are. A redskin heathen. A savage."

Rowena gasped at those words.

She looked at Tall Moon and saw fury in his eyes, yet he controlled his emotions and did not react openly.

"It is up to you," Tall Moon said, rising and yanking Darren to his feet. "It is all up to you."

He gave Darren a shove. "Get your horse," he said as he kicked dirt onto the campfire to put it out. "You are coming with me and Rowena whether or not you want to."

"I have no horse," Darren said thickly. "When I left, it was on foot."

"Do you think I did not know that?" Tall Moon said, laughing softly. "I just wanted to remind you of your loss. A man without a horse is a man without a heart.

"Follow me," Tall Moon went on, gesturing with one hand toward the trees where he and Rowena had left their horses. "We shall ride. You will follow on foot."

"What?" Darren said incredulously. "How . . . far . . . will you force me to walk?"

"Until we get where I am taking you," Tall Moon said, shrugging and not offering an exact answer.

From this moment on, his brother would have hell to pay. Perhaps he would even wish that he had fallen over that ledge to his death in the waters below.

Rowena glanced at Tall Moon. She smiled at him when he looked at her. "You planned this all along," she murmured. "While you were following his tracks, you knew what you would do when you found him."

"*Ho*, I knew," Tall Moon said, gazing at Darren, who only glared back. "*Ho*, brother, I knew your future before you even imagined I might catch you."

Rowena looked at Darren. "You should feel very fortunate that your brother has such a kind heart, for even though I know your next few days will be intolerable for you, he could very easily have allowed you to fall to your death."

"I wish now that he had," Darren mumbled, then winced as Tall Moon took some rope from his saddlebag and wrapped one end around Darren's wrists. He tied the other end to the pommel of his saddle and mounted his steed.

Rowena mounted her own.

She gave Darren a sly smile as he was made to follow behind both horses, on foot. Now that she understood Tall Moon's plan for his brother, she liked it!

Chapter Thirty

The morning sun was streaming through the cabin window as Rowena was awakened by the sound of someone easing down beside her on the bed of blankets and pelts.

She opened her eyes and smiled as Tall Moon swept an arm out and drew her closer to him as he lay down beside her.

She sighed with contentment.

She had slept soundly through the night, but she now recalled how she had at first had trouble dropping off to sleep. Tall Moon had lain beside her and told her that he would help her.

He had told her about a way to gain the serenity needed to drop off to sleep, how the Cherokee sang or repeated a prayer. He had then softly sung to her, the melody so beautiful and sweet, she had fallen peacefully asleep in his arms. She had dreamed of being with him, making love over and over again.

It had felt so real, she wondered now if it might have been.

Her skin seemed to tingle as he ran his hand down the curves of her body. For the first time in her life, Rowena had slept nude. She had only been nude one other time in her life in front of a man, and that had been when she and Tall Moon had made love.

She had felt bashful when he had gazed at her body then, touching her sweetly in places that became aroused immediately, places she had never known could react in such a way to anyone's touch.

But he wasn't just anyone.

He was the man she loved with all her heart. Anything he did to her made her feel a wondrous joy inside her heart.

"You slept well," he said, not as a question, but as a fact. "I have come and gone and you did not stir at all despite the noise I made while doing so. I even kissed you before I left—"

"You left?" Rowena asked, interrupting him. "You weren't here all night with me? I fell asleep in your arms. I have never been so exhausted in my life as I was last night."

"You had a trying day, but today . . . tomorrow . . . and the weeks and months ahead will be filled with happiness, for I will make it so," he said, brushing some fallen golden locks back from her brow.

Then he leaned forward and kissed the spot where her hair had just lain. "We will marry tomorrow," he said. "I have already spread the word among my people. Today, they will begin making arrangements for the celebration of love that we hold between us."

Rowena's eyes wavered. "I know that you are

your people's chief, but I am so afraid that many of them are not happy over your choice of wife," she murmured. "My skin . . . my hair . . . my eyes—"

"Are all beautiful," he said, interrupting her. "Now, my woman, do not fret because you look different from the Cherokee people. What lies inside, in your heart, is the important thing. You are a good person. Anyone who knows you sees that."

"But hardly any of your people know me," Rowena said, her voice breaking. "What if those who don't, who don't even want to know me, will never accept me?"

"I am their chief," Tall Moon said firmly. "They will never speak openly against you, and those who do not approve of you will soon see how wrong they are to have misjudged you. It will take time for some. But I do know that in time, all will love you."

"You smell so fresh and clean," Rowena said, changing the subject to a less stressful topic.

She reached up and stroked her fingers through his thick black hair. "And your hair is damp. Have you bathed in the river already this morning?"

"*Ho*," he said, his voice drawn. "It was necessary this morning more than most."

"Why?" Rowena asked.

"While you slept I went to gather up the roosters that were used in the cockfights, to bring them here. I hope they will become as tame as those that my people keep," Tall Moon said, his jaw tight. "When I got there, I saw that some were gone, for I know there were more than what I saw today."

"What do you think happened to them?"

Rowena asked, sitting up and drawing a blanket around her shoulders. "Did they get away on their own?"

"That would have been impossible, for the cages they were in are also gone," Tall Moon said, also drawing a blanket around his shoulders, for he had not yet started the morning fire. He had been too anxious to return to his bed, to be with Rowena.

"Do you mean someone went there and took them?" Rowena murmured.

"*Ho*, someone took them," Tall Moon said stiffly. "And those that were not taken were dead."

"Dead?" Rowena gasped. "Did someone kill them?"

"They apparently died from lack of water," Tall Moon said.

"When Darren hears about this, he will be fit to be tied," Rowena said, shuddering at the thought of how enraged Darren would be.

"He already knows," Tall Moon said dryly. "I told him as soon as I returned to the village."

"You did?" Rowena said, her eyes widening. "What did he say?"

"When he realized that someone had gone to the cabin and had taken some of the roosters, he was furious, more furious than when he heard that the others had died," Tall Moon said. He slowly kneaded his chin. "I heard him mention a name beneath his breath. Lloyd. He said the name Lloyd. He assumes that it was he who came and took some of the birds."

"Lloyd?" Rowena asked softly.

"I questioned Darren about him," Tall Moon said. "At first, he did not offer an answer. But when I persisted, he finally told me. Lloyd was a lumberjack under my father's employ. He is the one who was Darren's partner in the cockfights. He owned some of his roosters. The rest were Darren's. So it seems that Lloyd came and took his and left the rest to die."

"Why didn't he take them all?" Rowena murmured. "He must have known that if they weren't fed or watered soon, they would die."

"Darren said that he thought Lloyd would have been too afraid to steal Darren's roosters, for he knew my brother's temper," Tall Moon said.

"Yes, Darren's temper is frightening," Rowena murmured. "If he wasn't in one of your cabins and being guarded, you know that he would go after Lloyd. He would probably murder him if he found him and I truly don't think he would stop until he did find him."

"*Ho*, as easily as he murdered his own father," Tall Moon said, then started when someone spoke his name anxiously outside of the closed door.

It was Two Clouds, the warrior who had been told to stand guard outside Darren's cabin.

Tall Moon pulled on his breechclout again and slid his feet into moccasins, then handed a dress to Rowena. "While you slept, several women of my village came to me, offering dresses for you to wear," he said. "This is one of them. It is made of doeskin. Some of the others are to be worn on special days, such as our marriage; they are made of white doeskin. You will look beautiful in them all."

Rowena accepted the dress, admiring its beautiful beaded designs and the fringe around its hem.

"Dress while I go see what Two Clouds wants," Tall Moon said, then left the bedroom, closing the door behind him.

He went to the front door and opened it. When he saw the concern etched on his warrior's face, he knew that the news was not good.

Something made him look past Two Clouds, at the cabin where Darren had been taken. He saw the door was wide open.

"What has happened?" he asked. "What news have you brought me that makes you look so uncomfortable."

"While guarding your white brother, word came to me that my pregnant wife was suddenly ill," Two Clouds said, his dark eyes filled with apology. "I was too worried not to go see for myself how she was. While I was gone, your brother escaped."

"He is gone?" Tall Moon said, his voice tight with anger toward Two Clouds.

"He fled while I was gone and no one saw him leave," Two Clouds said, his voice breaking with emotion. "My chief, I am sorry, but I had to go to my wife. Our babe is coming, and it is too early. She or the child might not make it."

Seeing just how distressed Two Clouds was, and not wanting to put a heavier burden on this warrior's shoulders, Tall Moon reached a gentle hand to his arm. "Go and stay with your wife," he said, trying to keep the anger he felt out of his voice. "Send word to me later how she is faring."

"*A-a-do*, thank you, my chief, oh, thank you," Two Clouds said, turning and already running toward his cabin.

"Did my brother flee on foot, or did he steal a horse for his escape?" Tall Moon called out after Two Clouds.

He turned to Tall Moon. "No horses are gone," he said tightly. "I checked before coming to you. He has fled on foot."

Tall Moon nodded, then went back inside his cabin where Rowena waited for him.

"I heard," she murmured. "I can't believe Darren managed to do this. Just how far does he think he can get on foot? And he has no weapon. What does he think he will accomplish?"

"His hatred for Lloyd has blinded him," Tall Moon said. He slung his quiver of arrows on his back, then grabbed his bow. "I will go and find him."

"I want to go with you," Rowena said, hurrying with him toward the door.

Tall Moon stopped and turned to her.

He realized that she would feel better being with him than staying behind full of anxiety about what was happening, so he nodded.

"*O-ge-ye*, come," he said, taking her by the hand. "We must not waste any more time talking. Go and get our two horses while I study the tracks my brother left behind."

Rowena nodded and hurried to his corral.

She prepared both Misty and Magic, then took the reins and walked them from the corral. She led the horses to where Tall Moon was kneeling, studying the prints that led away from the cabin where Darren had been imprisoned.

Tall Moon nodded toward the woods. "He has gone that way. We will find him," he said as he mounted Magic. "He cannot have gotten far on foot."

They rode off together, Tall Moon's eyes following the signs of passage through the forest. It was soon evident where Darren was heading. Back to the arena where he had left his roosters.

"He is not thinking clearly," Rowena said when she realized where Darren was going. "What does he think he will achieve by going back to the cabin where he kept his roosters? You told him they were dead."

"I do not think he believed me," Tall Moon said tightly. "I imagine he thought I was just telling him that so he would forget about the roosters once and for all."

"But surely he knows you would not have left live roosters there," Rowena said, finding Darren's actions very strange.

"A man who would kill his own father is a man whose mind does not function as a normal person's would do," Tall Moon said, riding slowly onward. "He is a man driven by madness. His end will be one of pure misery."

Suddenly Rowena gasped, bringing her move to an abrupt stop. "There he is," she said, shuddering as she stared at Darren's body.

He lay on his back beneath a cypress tree, his eyes locked in a death stare. But it was the expression on his face that made Rowena shiver again. There was a look of terror in his eyes.

From this vantage point, she could see that he'd been horribly mauled by some forest creature. His body was twisted and torn, and blood covered the ground.

Tall Moon also drew rein and stared at his brother. There was a look of horror on Tall Moon's face.

"What do you . . . think . . . killed him?" Rowena asked, now turning her eyes away from the body.

"There are cougars that roam this forest. Without any weapon, my brother would have been helpless to defend himself," Tall Moon said, slowly dismounting.

He went and knelt beside his brother to take a closer look. Gently, he wiped the blood off Darren's face and closed his eyes.

"What are you going to do with his . . . body . . . ?" Rowena asked softly.

"Like all who die, no matter what their misdeeds while on this earth, he needs a final resting place," Tall Moon said, already gathering his brother's body up and carrying him toward his horse. "As his brother, I will see that is done for him."

"You will do that despite all the evil he did?" Rowena asked as Tall Moon laid his brother over the back of his horse, tying him to Magic.

"When he was born, he was innocent and good. That is what I will think about when I take him to his burial place," Tall Moon said thickly. "I will think about how much my mother would have loved him, were she to have lived. She would want her second-born given some kindness and love by his older brother."

Rowena marveled at his kindness, his gentleness toward someone who had caused him nothing but grief. But she had learned that everything Tall Moon did was motivated by the goodness of his heart, and she loved him even more for it.

"Where are you taking him . . . for . . . burial?" Rowena asked as he mounted Magic and took his reins in hand.

"To the cavern where we found him hiding," Tall Moon said, heading his horse in the direction of the cavern. Rowena followed alongside him on Misty.

"You aren't burying him in the ground?" she asked, recalling that he hadn't buried his father in the ground, either.

"There are ways of honoring the dead besides burial," Tall Moon said. "The cavern he chose while alive will be his final resting place in death."

They rode onward in silence and when they reached the cavern, Rowena stayed on her horse while Tall Moon took his brother inside. After several minutes had passed, she realized that he was taking much longer than she would have thought.

She supposed she should have realized that being a man of kind heart, Tall Moon would not just put his brother in the cavern and leave him without saying something meaningful over his body.

And then Tall Moon returned to his horse. He mounted Magic and turned to Rowena.

"I have done all that I can for a brother I truly never knew," he said, his voice drawn.

"You have done much more than most men would have done under the circumstances," Rowena said softly. "I am proud of you. I love you so much."

After riding a short distance, they entered a grove of tall cypress trees. At that moment they were startled to hear the sound of a cougar's cry.

"I believe that is the cougar that killed my brother," Tall Moon said. "Darren took pleasure in the deaths of many innocent creatures. Now he himself has died a violent death."

"It's almost as though nature has punished him for the evil he did," Rowena said, goose bumps rising on her arms.

"Yes, this forest can be a harsh place to those who do not understand or love it," Tall Moon said, shrugging. "My brother only wanted to cut its trees and take all he could from this place."

"Let's hurry home," Rowena said, her eyes wide as she continued to glance nervously around her.

"You are safe," Tall Moon said. "Because you are with me, my woman, you are safe, for always."

Chapter Thirty-one

Rowena could hardly believe that she was actually getting married today. She would not allow what had happened yesterday to ruin this joyful time for her.

This was hers and Tall Moon's special day, one that they would remember into old age, when both would have gray hair and wrinkles.

She was alone as she dressed. Tall Moon was waiting for her out in the front room of his cabin.

She had seen him already, dressed for the wedding ceremony. He was attired in a buckskin outfit beautifully decorated with beads. Today he wore his hair in two long braids down his back, with beads woven into the strands that matched the beading of his buckskin outfit.

Rowena thought he had never been as handsome as today. He took her breath away each time she looked at him.

And now he was going to be her husband!

She slipped the wedding dress over her head. It was the most beautiful white doeskin she had ever seen, and the beadwork on it matched the design that had been sewn on Tall Moon's. His cousin had made both garments.

Rowena wore no leggings. On her feet were doe-skin moccasins, again decorated with the same beadwork that was chosen for both her dress and Tall Moon's outfit.

Her long and flowing golden hair shone from a fresh washing and smelled of the forest and river. She had no mirror in which to see herself, but she could not help feeling beautiful.

Outside, she heard the women who had already gathered at the center of the village, where the wedding ceremony would be held. Some were shaking small gourds, while others sang and danced to the rhythmic beat of distant drums.

It was a beautiful early evening for the wedding. The late sun poured through the bedroom window close to where Rowena stood. She heard birds singing in the nearby forest.

Only yesterday she had found a nest of baby robins, with scarcely a feather on them. It was perhaps the mother that sang to them this evening.

"I hope soon I can give Tall Moon good news about our own tiny one," Rowena murmured to herself as she placed a hand on her belly.

She knew that she wasn't pregnant yet, but after tonight, yes, perhaps after tonight she could say that she was.

She had one more thing to do and then she would go to Tall Moon, ready to join hands with him as they walked outside, where his people awaited their chief and his chosen woman.

She took up a small bottle and shook a few

drops of liquid from it into the palm of her hand. She gently rubbed it along the inside of her arms.

Tall Moon had brought this to her early this morning, to wear on their wedding day.

It was perfume made of a mixture of plants, and particularly the petals of roses. The beautiful scent was supposed to cling to her skin all evening long, and into the night while she and her loved one would be making love.

"My husband . . ." she whispered.

This perfume was not like any other she had worn before . . . perfume her mother had actually ordered from Paris . . . but it was even sweeter than any of those her mother had paid so much money for.

Her mother had been an extravagant sort of person. Rowena didn't want to be that way. She just wanted to have a happy life. She needed no riches, no huge home, nothing more than this man she would soon call her husband and this cabin they would share together.

"Our home," she whispered, finding it hard to believe that so much had happened so quickly in her life since she had left the convent.

Meeting Tall Moon had been the best thing that had ever happened to her. She could hardly wait to begin their new life as husband and wife.

She pinched her cheeks in order to give them a rosier color. Then, sucking in a shaky breath, she opened the door to see Tall Moon patiently awaiting her in the front room.

When he turned, she saw a look of love in his

eyes that made her insides melt. She wondered if it would always be that way for her every time she saw him.

Up to now, it had!

"You are beautiful," Tall Moon said huskily as he went to her and took her hands in his. "My woman, I will love you *i-gs-hi-di*. I will love you forevermore."

"As I shall love you," Rowena murmured, their gazes holding. In each was a look of utter adoration for the other.

"As I have told you, the Cherokee marriage ceremony is not the same as the one you might know," he said softly. "If our parents were alive to participate in it, the ceremony would be more complex, but since they are not, it will be a very simple wedding. The ritual only includes the exchanging of blankets."

"Blankets?" Rowena asked, her eyes wide in wonder.

"The exchange of blankets symbolizes how we both will take on the duties of husband and wife in our Cherokee home," Tall Moon said softly. "We will go to the center of the village where blankets have been prepared for the ceremony by the women of my village. They will give them to us. We will then take them with us to our home. That will complete the ceremony. But my people will continue enjoying this special day long into the night, while we are alone and making love in our cabin."

"Our . . . cabin?" Rowena said, smiling softly. "I love the sound of that."

"Everything that is mine will be yours, my woman," Tall Moon said thickly.

"And no words will be spoken between us at the ceremony?" Rowena asked, searching his eyes.

"No words are needed to prove our love for each other," Tall Moon said, placing a gentle hand on her cheek. "They have already been said between us."

Suddenly Rowena heard something outside that made her heart skip a beat and her eyes widen. She looked quickly at the closed door, then up into Tall Moon's eyes.

"What is it?" he asked.

"It is something I am hearing," she said, again looking toward the closed door.

Had she actually heard a violin being played along with the drums and rattles? Where on earth could the Cherokee have gotten a violin? And why hadn't Tall Moon told her that they had one?

"What do you hear?" he asked, his eyes searching hers.

"A violin," she blurted out. "Someone is playing a violin."

"I do not know of such an instrument, although you have mentioned it more than once to me," Tall Moon said.

"But someone is playing one," she said, walking quickly to the door and opening it.

She gasped when she saw one of the men playing a violin. She looked quickly over her shoulder at Tall Moon. "Out there," she said, nodding toward those who were playing the instruments. "One of your men is playing a violin."

Still not sure what she could be talking about, he went to her and stood at her side. "Point it out to me," he said.

"There," she replied, pointing directly at the violin. "That man is playing a violin."

"No, he is playing a fiddle," Tall Moon said, giving her an incredulous look. "You do not know what a fiddle is?"

Finding it sweet that he did not know a fiddle and violin were one and the same, she smiled and gave him a kiss on the cheek. Then she turned to watch the man playing the violin again.

Although he was not playing the sort of music she had always played . . . symphony music . . . he was a fine musician.

She could hardly restrain herself from going out there and asking to play the instrument herself.

She turned to Tall Moon again. "Darling, the fiddle that the man is playing is also sometimes referred to as a violin," she said, smiling into his eyes. "The man playing it is quite talented."

"I did not know the instrument you told me about was the same as a fiddle," Tall Moon said; then he frowned. "And my brother broke it."

"And at the same moment broke my heart, for I adored my violin," Rowena murmured.

"I will tell my friend Long Bow what happened and ask him if he would mind letting you have his," Tall Moon said. "You see, this man makes violins. Either he can give you the one that is already made, or make you one. Which do you prefer?"

"I would not want to ask him to give his violin

to me," Rowena murmured. "I know how attached one gets to a particular instrument. I . . . would . . . not want him to feel the same loss that I felt when mine was taken from me."

"I would expect you to say nothing else," Tall Moon said, smiling into her eyes. "You are a woman of kind heart. I will ask Long Bow to make one for you that you can call your own. You two can play together. Would you do that for me and my people?"

"I would love to," Rowena said, her eyes filled with excitement. "My violin meant the world to me. When I played it, I could forget all the heartache and loneliness I felt after losing both my mother and father. Having a violin again would mean so much to me, and playing it with Long Bow would be wonderful."

"Then it is the same as done," Tall Moon said decisively. "You shall have your own violin and you can show your love for it as you play for my people."

"This is such a special day for me," Rowena said, tears filling her eyes. "I am to become the wife of a very special man and I will soon have a violin of my own again."

"Long Bow will feel honored to be able to make his chief's wife an instrument," Tall Moon said, smiling into her eyes.

"I will be so grateful and I look forward to playing a duet with Long Bow," Rowena replied, beaming.

"Duet?" Tall Moon asked. "What is this thing called . . . duet?"

"When two people play instruments at the same time, in harmony, that is a duet," Rowena said, smiling at him.

She was realizing that Tall Moon was unfamiliar with many customs of white people, even though his father had been white. But she loved this innocence about him and was glad that he had not spent his whole life with such a ruthless man as Lawrence Ashton.

Tall Moon might have turned out to be the same sort of person that his brother was, though she didn't see how that could have been possible. He was a man of such kindness, such warmth. That was not something learned. It was something that came from deep within one's soul.

She was suddenly aware of the silence outside, where the people awaited their chief and his woman.

Her heart began pounding. She had never been as anxiously happy as she was now, so happy it almost frightened her.

Surely something was going to happen to destroy this happiness. Hadn't that happened to her before? She had been so wondrously happy with her mother and father and they had suddenly been taken from her.

"Oh, Lord, please don't let it happen again," she prayed to herself as Tall Moon gently took one of her hands in his.

"Are you ready?" he asked, his eyes dancing.

"I am," Rowena murmured, knowing that her cheeks were flushed pink.

She was experiencing the happiest moment of

her life and did not want to think backward or forward. She just wanted to cherish the feeling.

"Walk beside me to the circle of people," Tall Moon said, moving beside her hand in hand, heart to heart, soul to soul.

Rowena was very aware of the silence that lay all around her. The only sounds now were the birds singing and chattering in the trees that fringed the village, and the river moving over stones not far from where the circle of people now stood.

Even the children were standing quietly beside their parents, their eyes following Tall Moon and Rowena until they stepped into the circle of people, then turned and faced each other.

The silence seemed complete now. Rowena no longer heard the birds, nor the splash of water.

All that she was aware of was the pounding of her heart and the sweetness she felt throughout her body as Tall Moon smiled and gazed into her eyes.

Several women approached. Two of them came closer, each holding a blanket. Without anyone saying anything, one blanket was handed to Tall Moon, the other to Rowena.

"We now return to our cabin," Tall Moon said, smiling down at Rowena, who gazed in wonder into his eyes.

As everyone watched, in silence and in awe that their chief had just taken a wife, Rowena and Tall Moon turned and walked back in the direction of his cabin. They were now man and wife!

Rowena loved the simplicity of the ceremony in

comparison to those she had witnessed back in the huge, tall white chapel in Atlanta.

She recalled how restless she had become as a small child while waiting for the long ceremonies to be over. It had always seemed that the minister would never stop talking before finally announcing the couple were husband and wife.

This evening, no one had had to say anything to join Tall Moon and Rowena in matrimony.

And now?

She and Tall Moon would join beneath those blankets and make sweet, sweet love!

Her heart pounded with each step as she got closer and closer to the cabin where she hoped one day to have many children blessing their home with laughter and love.

For this evening, she would be content to just be there with Tall Moon. They had so much loving to do. So much sharing.

She watched him out of the corner of her eye when they reached the closed door to the cabin.

She had read in novels that the husband carried the new bride across the threshold. Would Tall Moon know of such a practice?

She smiled to herself when he opened the door, then took her hand and led her inside, closing the door behind them.

That was enough for her. Being carried was just something someone had thought up.

Being here with Tall Moon, who was now her husband, was all that mattered.

With the door now closed behind them, both

laid their blankets aside, then moved into each other's arms.

"We are married," Tall Moon said, smiling into her eyes. "My woman, you are now my wife!"

The way he exclaimed it told Rowena just how much it meant to him that she was his wife.

"As you are now my husband," she said, sighing contentedly.

"And what do newly married people do?" Tall Moon demanded, a teasing light in his eyes.

"Well, now, I'm not altogether certain," Rowena teased back.

He suddenly swept her into his arms and carried her into the bedroom, where the bed was already prepared for the newlyweds, soft and beckoning.

As he slowly undressed her, he gazed into her eyes. "Because you are a chief's wife, you are now a woman of status," he said thickly.

"The only thing different about me is that I am happier, my love, than I ever thought possible," she murmured. "But I promise you that I will live up to what is expected of me as your wife."

With her dress now around her ankles on the floor, he removed her moccasins, leaving her fully nude before his feasting eyes.

"Undress me," Tall Moon said huskily.

Rowena smiled into his eyes, then watched as she revealed more and more of his flesh, until he was standing wonderfully nude before her.

Wanting to touch him, to feel his skin against her own, Rowena ran a hand slowly down his muscled chest, then across his flat belly, and then farther down to where his thickness filled her hand when she wrapped her fingers around him. She sighed, then moved her hand on him.

He closed his eyes and reveled in her touch, but when he felt himself getting too close to the brink, he opened his eyes and took her hand away.

He then traced her nakedness with his hands, touching her in places that he knew enhanced the passion she already felt.

When she began to tremble with ecstasy, he knew it was the moment when their bodies should be locked together in the most intimate way possible.

He held her as he pressed his body against hers, urging her down onto their bed of blankets and pelts.

"My love, my love," Rowena whispered against his lips as he joined their lips in a meltingly hot kiss while thrusting his manhood deep inside her.

"Never stop," Rowena whispered against his lips. "Love me, my darling. Love me."

Pleasure spread through her body with each thrust. She writhed in response and clung to him, soft moans repeatedly emerging from somewhere deep inside her.

She gave herself wholly to the rapture, as a raging hunger she had never felt before swept through her.

Tall Moon's lean, sinewy buttocks moved as he cradled her against him. The heat of passion was almost too much for him to bear as his body grew even more feverish.

They clung.

They rocked together in love's dance as waves of liquid heat pulsed through their locked bodies.

Breathing hard, his hands taking in the roundness of her breasts, kneading their soft fullness, Tall Moon buried his face in her neck. His hot breath against her flesh fired more desire inside Rowena.

She stroked his muscled back with both hands. They traveled lower. She sank her fingers into his buttocks, holding him more tightly against her. She wrapped her legs around him and rode him, giving more power to his manhood as it now reached even deeper into her heat, touching her where he had not been before.

This brought gasps of pleasure from Rowena.

She was a flood of emotions, groaning in pleasure with each of his thrusts inside her. The euphoria that filled her was almost too much to bear.

She moaned as he kissed her again, and gave in to total rapture as it rose up inside her, spreading and swelling, until it blotted out everything but the wonder of how this man could make her body react.

"I cannot hold off any longer," Tall Moon said huskily against her lips. "My body. It is aching from my need to fully have you. Are . . . you . . . feeling the same?"

"Yes, please take me with you to paradise," Rowena whispered back to him, arching her back. Her body tightened against his as he thrust inside her, over and over again, until they both reached the ultimate of pleasure.

Their bodies strained together. Their breaths mingled as they again kissed.

Both were left shaken, their skin tingling still from what they had found in each other's arms.

Tall Moon's body now stilled against Rowena's. He cradled her face between his hands and gazed adoringly into her passion-clouded eyes. "I shall always want you as fiercely as I did tonight," he said, smiling. "My wife, my woman, you are my shining star. Our life together will be one of sheer ecstasy."

Again he kissed her, sending wild ripples of desire through Rowena anew.

He entered her again, and though she had so recently found ecstasy in his arms, she could feel it building again. . . .

Chapter Thirty-two

Many years later—autumn

The land of the Cherokee was aflame with the colors of autumn; the scarlet of the maple trees and the gold of birch and cottonwood.

The harvest had been good for the Bird Clan of Cherokee this autumn, and the fish from the river had been bountiful.

Today had been an especially good day.

Rowena and Tall Moon had gone fishing in their family canoe with their two children, a son named Running Pony, and a daughter named Sweet Moon. A huge bass had been caught and would soon be cooked for supper.

But for now, Tall Moon sat before the fireplace in a thickly cushioned chair and filled his pipe with tobacco.

Rowena sat on the opposite side of the fireplace from Tall Moon. The fire's glow on her face revealed her contentment.

She paused in sewing a dress for her daughter and gazed at Tall Moon. She was still as struck by his handsomeness as she had been on the first day she had seen him.

And she loved the way he puffed on his pipe, drawing rich tobacco smoke into his mouth, then slowly exhaling it as he stared at the fire, seemingly lost in his own thoughts.

Her golden hair was drawn back from her face to hang in one long braid down her back. She wore a plain buckskin dress, saving the more beautiful ones for special occasions.

She gazed beyond Tall Moon at the changes she had brought to his home. It had comfortable furniture now, kerosene lamps that glowed warm with fire, and a braided carpet made by Rowena's own hands.

The women of the village had taught her how to make the rug, for many of the Cherokee people had the same in their own homes.

A kitchen had been added on, with a cast-iron stove. In it was an apple pie, and the smudges of flour on Rowena's face were proof that she had made it herself.

The children had picked the apples, Tall Moon had peeled them, and Rowena had done the rest. Her family loved pie as a special dessert.

Rowena was proud to have adapted well to Tall Moon's way of life, just as he had adjusted to what she had brought into the marriage.

She knew the Cherokee language well and could speak it, herself. She loved hearing the clan speaking in their Cherokee tongue, for their language was so soft and beautiful.

Earlier in the evening Rowena had brought dried locust pods from storage and had made a sweet drink from them for her family, which they all loved. The only drink Tall Moon preferred was a kind of beer made out of persimmons.

He drank this on special occasions, as he had on the two days of his children's births. He had shared it with his warriors, who celebrated with him and Rowena. Every child was welcomed by the Cherokee, for each child born to the their people helped to build a stronger Bird Clan.

Her thoughts were interrupted when her daughter came into the room, her violin and bow held in her hands.

"Mama, Papa, may I show you what I have learned today?" Sweet Moon asked, causing everyone to look her way, even her brother, who sat on a chair, reading by lamplight.

"Most certainly, you can play for us," Tall Moon said, tapping the tobacco from his pipe into the fireplace. He smiled at Rowena. "Shining Star, I see such pride in your eyes. I know how happy you are that your daughter loves the violin as you love it."

Rowena returned his smile. She adored the Indian name, which had been given to her by her husband the first night of their marriage. Shining Star.

"I am so very, very proud of our daughter's skill with the violin," she murmured, then glanced over her shoulder at her son, who seemed more interested in books than riding and hunting with the other children his age.

Rowena knew Running Pony's interests had begun to worry Tall Moon. He loved his son no matter what, but Running Pony was next in line to be chief and needed to know all of the things that children his age knew and enjoyed.

Tall Moon had often told Rowena in bed at night, when both children were asleep in their own rooms, that hunting skills could not come from a book.

She gave Tall Moon a look that told her husband to be patient with a son who was his exact image in skin, hair, and eyes. Already Running Pony was showing his father's handsomeness.

Tall Moon nodded and turned his attention back to his daughter. "Let us hear what you have learned to play today," he said, giving her a soft smile.

As she began playing, Rowena again became lost in thought. Long Bow had made her the very violin her daughter was playing, and she loved having it.

But her daughter had more time to use it now. Rowena was kept busy with her wifely and motherly duties. Rowena had taught Sweet Moon how to play, and the entire village was enchanted by the music.

Word had been received that white settlers were building homes not far from their village, but so far, no one had come to trouble the Bird Clan. She hoped it stayed that way.

She had never been able to understand how her own government could have been so aggressive and unkind in the past toward people such as these. All the Cherokee wanted out of life was to be able to like peacefully with their families.

Rowena prayed often that the people of this

village, whom she loved so dearly, could continue to live as happily as they were living now.

Tall Moon did not know it, but one day when he was gone on a long hunt, Rowena had gone into one of the new towns that were springing up nearby. She had met with the mayor of this town. She had explained to him how it was with the Cherokee people of the Bird Clan, that they were peace-loving and would never cause trouble for whites.

As it happened, the man she had spoken with had been a neighbor in Atlanta, one who came often and visited with her father. His name was Virgil Pfluegger. Before the war, Virgil and her father had been the best of friends.

She knew that Virgil could be trusted. In fact, Virgil planned to come one day soon and meet with her husband.

That day Rowena would be the one playing the violin, for Virgil had recalled hearing her play while visiting her father, and asked if she would be so kind to play for him again when he came to meet with Tall Moon. She had assured him that she would be more than happy to oblige.

Sweet Moon's song was now over. Tall Moon smiled when she tucked the violin beneath her left arm, as she'd been taught by Rowena, and slowly bowed.

"Wonderful!" Rowena cried, clapping along with her son and husband. "Bravo! We want to hear more."

Happy to oblige without being asked twice, Sweet Moon began playing another song.

Rowena smiled at Tall Moon, then at Running Pony. She was filled with contentment.

Ho, life was beautiful.

Life was wonderful.

She would never allow herself to wonder how it would have been had she not gone to live with Lawrence Ashton.

A world without Tall Moon and her children would be a world of emptiness.

And she would do everything within her power, as a white woman married to a powerful chief, to keep life peaceful and wonderful for the people who had welcomed her with opened arms. She would stand beside Tall Moon as his shining star, helping him for the rest of their lives.

Dear Reader,

I hope you enjoyed reading *Savage Sun*. The next book in my Savage series, which I am writing exclusively for Leisure books, is *Savage Dawn*. This book is filled with much romance, excitement and a few surprises.

Those of you who are collecting my Indian romance novels, and want to know more about the series and my entire backlist of Indian books, can check out www.dorchesterpub.com. Thank you for your support of my Indian series. I love writing about our nation's beloved Native Americans, our country's true first people.

Always,
Cassie Edwards

Turn the page for an exciting preview of
TUMBLEWEED
by award-winning author
JANE CANDIA COLEMAN

Allie Earp always said the West was no place for sissies. And that held especially true for a woman married to one of the wild Earp brothers. She had no fear of cussing a blue streak if someone crossed her, patching up a bullet wound, or defending her home against rustlers. Every day was a new adventure—from the rough streets of Deadwood to the infamous OK Corral in Tombstone. But through it all one thing remained constant: her deep and abiding love for one of the most formidable lawmen of the West.

Chapter One

I was too young to know that nothing ever stays the same, that sooner or later the world finds you. I was four, maybe five, when the Kansas-Nebraska Act brought trouble right to our doorstep. All of a sudden there was death in the air and folks shouting words I didn't understand—Abolition, state's rights, slavery—and Mum kept the shotgun by the door when Pa was out in the field. We didn't get the shooting and hanging Kansas did, but wagons headed there went through Omaha, some even through our pasture, and always there was night riders up to no good.

"It'll come to war," Pa said one night when we was at supper. The light in the lamp flickered when he spoke, and all of a sudden he looked old.

It scared me. Like I was seeing the future, seeing change, and helpless to stop it.

Mum sighed. "Seems it's already war here. All these folks coming and ready to fight. What'll happen to us?"

"I don't know. I wish I did. But the day anybody brings slaves to Nebraska is the day I start my own fight."

"What's slaves?" I asked, although us kids weren't supposed to interrupt our parents.

Pa stared across the table at me. "It's one man ownin' another. Or a lot of others. And it's wrong."

I thought about that. "Like we own Sally?" Sally was our cow.

"You might say that. 'Cept men ain't animals, and Sally's treated better than some of the slaves I heard about."

By the time us kids crawled into bed, my five-year-old mind was running off in all directions. "I don't want nobody ownin' me," I whispered to Melissa.

She giggled. "You will one day. When you're grown."

"I won't, either." Growing up to me meant trouble.

"Anyhow"—she gave a big yawn—"folks like us ain't slaves, and we sure don't own any. Now go to sleep."

"What if there's a war? Will we get to fight, too?"

"It's men who do the fightin'. Women stay home and worry."

"I bet I could fight good as a man," I said. "Even if I am a girl."

"And if you don't hush talkin', you'll be a sorry one." She turned over, her back to me.

"You ain't my boss," I mumbled, but she didn't answer, and I lay there, hearing all the night sounds—Pa snoring on the other side of the quilt that divided the rooms, the wind in the leaves of the big cottonwood, an owl calling from the creek bottom.

One thing I knew for sure. I didn't want anybody bossing me. Not then, not ever. What I didn't understand was that, when you love somebody, there's no question of who owns who or who gives orders.

That's what I was thinking when Virge found me later that night, a long ways from camp. My feet had taken me up the big wash to where the hills turned rocky, and the trees thinned out.

"I thought you'd got lost." He put his good arm around me, and I leaned up against him.

"Lost!" I said. "All you men can think of is a woman who can't find her way in the dark. I was just rememberin' back."

He shook his head. "Seems we never stop talking about that place. We're marked. Like Cain. I wish we'd never left the farm. Or stayed in Prescott. Had a family instead of followin' some pipe dream." He sounded bone-tired.

"Spilt milk," I told him.

"I'm not cryin'."

"I know that."

The Earp men didn't waste time on tears. That was left to us women, but, if we cried, we did it alone where no one could see. The faces we showed were masks, but I reckon everybody does that—hide behind a smile or a pokerface. You're safest that way.

I put my arm around Virge's waist. "Let's go on back. Let's go to bed."

His laugh began down low. I could feel it moving up into his chest. "You got somethin' in mind, Allie?"

"How'd you guess?"

The laugh spilled out, big and jolly, Virge's laugh. "Because I know you down to your toes."

And that's a comfort. Being understood and no need to play games. But being me, I had to have the last word. "That's what you think," I said.

Discover Great Native American Romance

If you crave the turbulent clash of cultures and the heat of forbidden love, don't miss these exciting Native American Romances:

Chosen Woman by Shirl Henke
Coming July 2009

When Fawn meets rough-and-tumble Jack Dillon, she is both infuriated by his cocky self-confidence and irresistibly drawn to his charismatic charm. He is the wolf totem of her dreams and holds the key to unlocking her visionary powers. Together they can save her people, if only he chooses to love her.

Comanche Moon Rising by Constance O'Banyon
Coming August 2009

Struggling to make a new life for herself and her young brother on a rugged ranch in Texas, Shiloh finds an unlikely protector in the chief of a nearby band of Comanches. But when he kidnaps them, she is torn between outrage and the powerful attraction she feels for the virile warrior.

Black Horse by Veronica Blake
Coming October 2009

Adopted by the Sioux as a young child, Meadow thinks of herself as one of the People, until a white visitor to their camp notices her pale coloring and begins questioning her background. When torn from the only home she's ever known, a virile young chief must risk his freedom to rescue her.

"Mega fun, fast-paced and with a sexy to-die-for hero—
my favorite kind of historical romance."
—Lori Foster

LISA COOKE

Texas Hold Him

As if losing the war to the Yankees hadn't been bad enough, Lottie Mason now needed $15,000 to keep her ailing father out of prison. The only place she could think of to get that kind of money was a riverboat poker tournament. Problem was, she didn't know a thing about playing cards.

Dyer Straights may have been the best cardsharp in New Orleans, but the true goal of this hardened gunslinger was vengeance, not profit. He didn't have time for a beautiful belle who wouldn't take no for an answer. So to scare her off, he upped the ante with a proposition: He'd give her the lessons she was so desperate for. And if she won the jackpot, she'd owe him one naked night in his bed. He didn't realize she couldn't afford to refuse.

As the cards are dealt and the seduction deepens, the two find they're taking a gamble on a lot more than a good hand and a one-night stand—they're betting on a lifetime of love.

ISBN 13: 978-0-8439-6254-3

RUNAWAY

New York Times bestselling author

Bobbi Smith

Running Scared

Destiny Sterling had to get away from St. Louis. Otherwise she'd never escape her stepfather's hot hands...or his hideous plans for her. Her only hope was to pose as a mail-order bride traveling to Texas to marry a rancher.

Running from the Law

Dan Cooper was as low-down mean as they came. He took pride in his gang's rough reputation...and the string of successful robberies they'd pulled off. His ace in the hole was a remote Texas ranch where he planned to lie low if things got too hot.

Running the Show

Texas Ranger Lane Madison knew the Cooper gang would show up at the Sundown Ranch sooner or later. All he had to do was play the part of its new owner...and wait. What he didn't count on was having to marry a vulnerable young beauty to keep up the role, or the inescapable attraction that made any secret between them impossible.

"Nobody does a Western better than Bobbi Smith."
—*Romantic Times BOOKreviews*

ISBN 13: 978-0-8439-6281-9

Bonnie Vanak

"…[writes] thrilling adventures, clever plots and unforgettable characters!"
—*Romantic Times BOOKreviews*

NOBLE IN ALL BUT NAME

Anne Mitchell, born illegitimate and raised in a work-house, sold by her mother and packed off by her father to the East, had every reason to lose faith. But in Egypt she found identity with the Khamsin, a tribe of Bedouin warriors. Greater even than the secret they entrusted to her was her newfound honor, and for that she would give all.

NOBLE IN ALL BUT ACTION

Nigel Wallenford was an earl. He was also a thief, a liar and a libertine. Regaining his birthright of Claradon had been a start. Next he required wealth, and he knew of just the fabled treasure…and its key's guardian was a ripe fig waiting to be plucked. Never before had he scrupled to cheat, steal or even murder. One displaced Englishwoman, no matter how fair, would hardly be his match.

The Lady & the Libertine

ISBN 13: 978-0-8439-5976-5

☐ **YES!**

Sign me up for the Historical Romance Book Club and send my FREE BOOKS! If I choose to stay in the club, I will pay only $8.50* each month, a savings of $6.48!

NAME: _____

ADDRESS: _____

TELEPHONE: _____

EMAIL: _____

☐ I want to pay by credit card.

☐ **VISA** ☐ **MasterCard.** ☐ **DISCOVER**

ACCOUNT #: _____

EXPIRATION DATE: _____

SIGNATURE: _____

Mail this page along with $2.00 shipping and handling to:
Historical Romance Book Club
PO Box 6640
Wayne, PA 19087
Or fax (must include credit card information) to:
610-995-9274
You can also sign up online at **www.dorchesterpub.com**.
*Plus $2.00 for shipping. Offer open to residents of the U.S. and Canada only.
Canadian residents please call 1-800-481-9191 for pricing information.
If under 18, a parent or guardian must sign. Terms, prices and conditions subject to change. Subscription subject to acceptance. Dorchester Publishing reserves the right to reject any order or cancel any subscription.